dish

#6

On the Back Burner

friends, cooking, eating, talking, life.

Grosset & Dunlap

dish #6

On the Back Burner

friends, cooking, eating, talking, life.

By Diane Muldrow

Illustrated by Barbara Pollak

Grosset & Dunlap
New York

For Lauren Roth—D.M.

Text copyright © 2003 by Diane Muldrow. Illustrations copyright © 2003 by Barbara Pollak. All rights reserved. Published by Grosset & Dunlap, a division of Penguin Putnam Books for Young Readers, 345 Hudson Street, New York, NY, 10014. GROSSET & DUNLAP is a trademark of Penguin Putnam Inc. Published simultaneously in Canada. Printed in the U.S.A.

Library of Congress Cataloging-in-Publication Data is available.

ISBN 0-448-42897-0   A B C D E F G H I J

"**S**urprise!"

Stunned, Natasha Ross faced the blurry crowd of people who filled the Moores' living room. This couldn't be for her! Could it?

Molly and Amanda Moore came forward and hugged her. "Happy birthday!" Molly sang out in a loud voice, her high, brown ponytail swinging.

Molly's identical twin, Amanda, squeezed Natasha's shoulders. "Are you surprised?" she asked.

"Totally! Surprised is not the word. I'm shocked! How did you—What about—We're not cooking tonight?" Natasha had thought she was coming over to the Moore's house for a last-minute cooking job for their business, Dish. But instead of finding the other members of Dish—Molly and Amanda Moore, Shawn Jordan, and Peichi Cheng—wearing aprons in the kitchen, they were standing in the living room in front of a table filled with food and presents. Purple and silver streamers hung from the ceiling, and there were little twinkle lights hanging in the windows. A bright flash from a camera caught Natasha's eye, and she saw her parents standing in a corner with Mrs. Moore, taking pictures and beaming at her.

Peichi joined Natasha and the twins. "*You're* not cooking!" She giggled. "This afternoon we got everything ready. We made all of your favorites— hummus and baba ghanouj, caramel popcorn, even deep-dish pizza with broccoli and pepperoni!"

"*And* angel food cake with fresh strawberries and whipped cream!" exclaimed Amanda. "Believe me, it is *not* easy to find really yummy, fresh strawberries in Brooklyn in January!"

"Wow!" Natasha said. "You guys are good!"

"We don't miss much," Shawn agreed. "Maybe we should open up a combination cooking and party-planning business! Dish Parties: We bring the food *and* the fun!"

"Forget it," Molly said, laughing. "We're busy enough as it is. We don't need *more* to do."

"That's for sure," Natasha agreed. They'd been *really* busy ever since starting Dish the previous summer. It all began when Amanda, Molly, and Shawn signed up to take cooking classes at Park Terrace Cookware. The girls were surprised to see Peichi and Natasha in the same class. They liked Peichi, even though they didn't know her very well then, but Natasha was another story. At the time, Natasha was Molly, Amanda, and Shawn's enemy, and it looked as though she might make the cooking class *really* unpleasant for them. However, the twins were determined not to let her ruin it for them. Their mom encouraged them to be nice to Natasha and see what happened, and it worked—Natasha started being nicer to them, too.

When their friend and classmate Justin McElroy's kitchen was destroyed by a small electrical fire, the twins' mom suggested that the girls help her cook some food for the McElroy family to help them through such a difficult time. The girls loved spending the entire day cooking and decided to start a cooking club called Dish. After Mrs. Moore saw what a great job they did cooking for the McElroys, she hired them to cook a week's worth of meals while she was at a conference in California. From there, the girls decided to turn their club into a business, cooking tasty, healthy meals for families who were too busy to cook during the week. In Natasha's opinion, Dish was the best thing that could have happened to her. Cooking with Amanda, Molly, Shawn, and Peichi was the most fun she'd ever had.

"Ready for one of your gifts?" Peichi asked Natasha. She pulled Natasha over to the couch. Mrs. Ross, still holding her camera, sat down in a chair across from the couch. It looked like she was planning to stay and take more pictures as Natasha opened her presents! *Oh, no,* thought Natasha. *It will be sooo embarrassing if she stays and takes pictures!*

Mr. Ross saw the look on his daughter's face and came

forward. "I guess that's our cue, Natalie," he said to Natasha's mom. He turned to Natasha. "Don't worry, sweetheart," he said with a smile. "We're heading out. We just wanted to see your face when the girls yelled 'surprise!' " He gave Natasha a kiss. Natasha gave her dad a smile that said, *Thanks for understanding, Dad!*, then looked warily at her mom. Natasha was relieved to see that her mom was putting on her coat. The camera was safely stored away in its bag. Mrs. Ross looked like she wanted to stay a little longer, but instead she also kissed Natasha and said, "I packed your overnight bag. Have a wonderful time at your party! We'll see you in the morning."

"I'll walk you to the door," Mrs. Moore said, leaving the room with the Rosses.

"So how does it feel to be twelve?" Peichi asked Natasha. "It definitely sounds more...*adult* than eleven!"

"It feels *great!*" Natasha said with a big smile. "You guys, this is the coolest birthday ever," she said. "Thank you so much."

"Let's get to the presents!" said Amanda eagerly. Natasha sat on the couch with Amanda on one side and Molly on the other. Although they were identical twins with freckles, long brown hair, and bright green eyes, everyone could easily tell them apart. Molly's high ponytail and casual clothes were her trademark look. Tonight Molly was wearing her favorite jeans and a forest-green sweater that made her bright green eyes look even greener than usual. Amanda, who was wearing a teal scoop-neck top with four thin silver necklaces, a straight black skirt, and the new boots she had gotten for Christmas, was much more fashion-conscious. She loved reading the latest fashion magazines and was always experimenting with different hairdos and outfits.

Shawn brought Natasha her first present. It was neatly wrapped in paper covered with sparkling stars, streaking comets, and planets. "Nice paper," Natasha observed, tucking her chin-length blond hair behind her ears.

"It foretells what's inside," Peichi said mysteriously as she perched on the arm of the sofa.

Natasha lifted the package. "Hmmm...it's so heavy, it must be moon rocks! Or maybe an asteroid!"

"Close!" Shawn said.

"Close?" Natasha questioned, laughing. "How could that be close?"

"Our fortunes lie in the stars!" Peichi hinted. "You'll see. Just open it already!" The girls were *really* excited.

Beneath the paper was a thick hardcover book. Lifting it, Natasha read the title aloud. "*What's Your Sign? A Cosmic Guide for Young Astrologers.*"

Her friends were all staring at her, smiling. "Cool, isn't it?" Shawn said.

"*Very* cool! Thanks," Natasha said.

The doorbell rang and her four friends grinned. "How perfect is that!" Amanda exclaimed and then ran to get the door.

"Who else is coming?" Natasha asked, looking at her friends. But they just smiled mysteriously and said nothing.

Amanda returned quickly with a middle-aged woman whose thick, brown curls cascaded down the front of her purple peasant dress. Her arms were adorned with a row of bangle bracelets and she wore large silver hoop earrings. "Meet Sonia," Amanda said, stretching her arm out dramatically to present the woman. "She's a licensed astrologer—*and* a psychic! We saw her ad tacked to the bulletin board at Park Terrace Cookware."

Sonia waved to them. "Hi, girls! Ready to unlock the secrets of your futures?"

Molly, Natasha, and Shawn exchanged anxious glances. Were they ready? They weren't sure. Knowing the future might be a little scary.

"Yes, of course we are," Amanda broke the silence. After all, she figured, they'd already paid Sonia to tell fortunes at this party. There was no sense wasting time. "Natasha should go first," Amanda said, "since she's the birthday girl."

The girls followed Amanda over to an upholstered chair and side table that Amanda had decorated with shawls and velvety pillows. She had even hung beaded curtains to partition this part of the living room from the rest of the house. "You sit here, Sonia," she said, indicating the big chair. Then she pulled over a straight back chair that she'd draped with a lace tablecloth. "And Natasha, you sit here."

"Very nice," Sonia said as she sat down and reached into her large, upholstered carpetbag. She pulled out a smoky crystal ball and carefully placed it on the table.

"Do real psychics actually use those?" Peichi whispered to Shawn. Shawn just shrugged and watched as Natasha cautiously sat across from Sonia.

Sonia studied Natasha seriously for nearly a minute before speaking. "You were born on January thirteenth, which makes you a Capricorn. People born under this sign are usually cautious and aware of what others think of them," she began. "They are hardworking, able to get things done quickly, and gifted with good memories."

"This is all so true!" Natasha cried.

"Let me see your palm, please," Sonia requested. Natasha placed her palm in Sonia's outstretched hand. Usually Natasha didn't believe in astrology and palm reading, but today she *wanted* to believe. Believing made it more fun—and spookier, too.

"*Ahhh*," Sonia said as she traced her nail up a crease

in Natasha's palm. It tickled a little. "Interesting," Sonia murmured.

"What?" Amanda asked eagerly, unable to control her curiosity another minute. "What's in her future?"

"See how the lines of your hand converge here at this point?" Sonia said to Natasha. "This indicates fame." Sonia pulled the crystal ball toward her and gently laid her hand on it. She exhaled slowly.

Natasha's free hand flew to her chest. "Me? Famous?" Her eyes widened happily. "I bet I'll write something that will win awards. I'll be an award-winning journalist!" Natasha wrote for the school newspaper, *The Post*.

"No," Sonia said. "I see something more active here. It is something you are doing—something millions of people will watch."

"Uh-oh," Natasha said, starting to worry. "I hope I don't get famous for having an accident or something, and end up on the six o'clock news!"

"No, no, no," Sonia assured her. "No accident. Don't worry so much. This is good fame. Is it for being in the movies? It could be...No, I see something similar, but smaller...There are lights...Yes! TV! You will be a TV star. Millions will watch you...You will shine."

Amanda's eyes popped open. *No way!* she thought to herself. Amanda was the one who was interested in acting. If anyone in their group of friends would turn out to be the TV star, Amanda was sure that *she* would be the one. She opened her mouth to say something, but caught Molly giving her "the look." *Uh-oh*, Amanda thought. She didn't want to offend Natasha, but...

"But you're not interested in acting, are you, Natasha?" Amanda asked impulsively, ignoring Molly's look. "I mean, I never heard you say you were and you don't try out for the plays or anything like that."

"No, Amanda, you're totally right!" Natasha exclaimed. "I've never been in a play and I've never wanted to be! I would be *so* nervous!"

Sonia stared at Natasha's palm. Then she squeezed Natasha's hand lightly and shut her eyes, obviously concentrating. "Yes, it is definitely TV. I see you there very clearly." She opened her eyes and nodded, satisfied with her prediction.

"Okay, if you say so," Natasha said. She stood up slowly. Natasha was relieved that her turn was over and that her fortune hasn't been a negative one, but she had a funny feeling...like she wanted to know more.

"Who wants to go next?" Sonia asked, looking up at the girls.

"I do!" Peichi said. "My birthday is November twenty-third."

"Ah, Sagittarius, such bright, funny people," Sonia said. "Sagittarians are very honest. Sometimes that causes a problem when they are so honest that they don't take the feelings of others into consideration. Be careful not to be so blunt that you offend those around you."

"Well, if people can't handle the truth, that's not *my* problem," Peichi said with a laugh.

Sonia smiled. "See what I mean? You are a true Sagittarian. Let me see your palm, please." Peichi presented her hand, palm up, and Sonia inspected it. "Change is coming. *Big* change. It's here very clearly," she predicted.

"What kind of change?" Peichi asked eagerly.

"I don't know exactly," Sonia admitted. "Possibly there will be a new addition to your house."

"We just got a new pool last summer," Peichi joked. "What's next, a tennis court?"

"Awesome!" Molly cheered. "A tennis court would be great."

"Or maybe a whirlpool," Amanda suggested. "I'd like you to get one of those."

"I'll let my parents know," Peichi replied, laughing. She stood up from the chair.

"Me next," Shawn said, slipping into the chair as soon as Peichi had gotten up. Her brown eyes shone with excitement behind her purple cat glasses. "I'm April sixteenth."

"Aries!" Sonia said. "You are very active, aren't you?"

"That's true. I'm a cheerleader!" Shawn told her.

"You are also brave, confident, and determined," Sonia added.

"That's *definitely* true! I was scared to try out for

cheerleading, but I did it anyway, which I guess was pretty brave. Once I tried out I felt pretty confident I'd make the team, and I *did* make it! I practice really hard because I'm determined to be really good. Angie always says that if I keep practicing this hard, I could be one of the best on the team next year." Amanda rolled her eyes as Shawn rambled on and on about cheerleading.

"Well, Aries loves a compliment," Sonia said, laughing lightly. When she looked at Shawn's palm, her expression grew serious again. "There are changes coming for you, too. You will worry about losing someone's love. But no matter who does the cooking, you will always be the apple of your father's eye."

Shawn stared at her with a bewildered expression. What did *that* mean? It was eerie that Sonia had mentioned her father. A few years ago, Shawn's mother had died after a long illness. Shawn's grandmother and cousins lived in South Carolina and she loved them very much, but since Shawn was an only child, she sometimes felt like her father was all she had. And it was almost creepy that Sonia had mentioned cooking—how could she have possibly known that the girls had a cooking business? "What's that about the cooking?" Shawn asked. "Why did you say that?"

"I mentioned cooking because food has something to do with what will happen in your future," Sonia replied. "Cooking food is important somehow."

"That's strange. It sounds like it must be true, but I can't imagine what it could mean," Shawn said, thinking hard. "I mean, it just doesn't make sense to me."

"Can Amanda and I go next?" Molly asked.

Sonia's brow furrowed as she thought. "It's unusual to do a reading for more than one person at a time, but seeing as you're twins..." she began.

Amanda didn't give her a chance to finish, but sat down next to Molly. "We were born on May twenty-seventh," the twins said at the same time. They giggled. "The twin thing!" That's what the twins called it whenever they said or thought the same thing at the same time, which happened pretty often.

"That makes you Geminis," Sonia said, smiling. "How perfect—twins born in the sign of the twins. Geminis can be moody, unpredictable, athletic, independent, and they usually don't make up their minds easily."

"That's weird," Shawn said. "Amanda can be moody and has a hard time making up her mind, and Molly is the one who's athletic and independent. They've split the Gemini traits between them."

"Hey, how come you gave me all the bad traits?" Amanda complained to Shawn.

"Those traits aren't really good or bad," Sonia said. "They're just tendencies. Moodiness can indicate deep sensitivity or strong creativity."

"I am very sensitive," Amanda said thoughtfully. "And being an actress really requires creativity. This is so cool!

What will my future hold?" She presented her palm for Sonia to inspect. Sonia bit her lip as she looked at Amanda's palm. It almost looked like she was frowning, but Amanda couldn't quite tell because her face was down. It made Amanda nervous. What was Sonia seeing in her future? "What?" Amanda finally demanded. "What do you see?"

Sonia sighed. "I am seeing that in the not-to-distant future you will be faced with a difficult event. It will be a very hard time for you. You will feel like you are losing your best friend," she said softly.

Amanda sat back, stunned. She was sure she knew *exactly* what Sonia was talking about. Shawn had been best friends with Molly and Amanda ever since the three of them were small. But, since last summer, their friendship had changed. No matter what the twins did to stay close to Shawn, Shawn seemed more distant—especially since she'd made the cheerleading squad. Actually, Amanda had tried out for cheerleading, too—mostly to be close to Shawn. But only Shawn had made the team.

Now Amanda was glad she hadn't made cheerleading. Angie Martinez was on the team, and she was Amanda's least favorite person in the world. Angie was really nasty to Shawn's other friends, particularly Amanda, and it made Amanda furious. Shawn wished that *all* of her friends would get along, but it was starting to seem like that would never happen.

"I already feel like I'm losing a best friend," Amanda said quietly—so quietly that no one heard her. She got up and moved away from the table.

"You are also a Gemini," Sonia said as she turned to Molly, "so you've already heard all about that. Let's see what your future holds." Molly presented her palm. "*Hmmmm,*" Sonia murmured. Once again, her face darkened. "I see heartbreak here. Not your heart, though. You will cause someone's heart to break. Your sister?"

"No way!" Molly cried. She would never hurt Amanda.

"Yes, it is your sister," Sonia insisted.

"That will never happen," Natasha told Sonia. "Molly and Amanda are too tight for that."

Sonia shrugged. "This is what I see. It is your choice whether or not you believe it."

The room fell silent.

Oh, great, thought Amanda. *First I lose my best friend, now my sister's going to break my heart? This fortune-telling thing was such a bad idea.* She turned to the rest of the group. "Well, this is all make-believe, anyway," she said with a bright smile. "I'm gonna put our pizzas in the oven." She quickly turned and went to the kitchen. The rest of the girls looked at Sonia, a little embarrassed. But Sonia just smiled.

"She really *is* a Gemini—a moody one!" Sonia said lightly. The girls laughed. Then Sonia's voice turned serious. "None of you should be upset by what I've said tonight. Please, tell your sister that," Sonia said, turning to Molly. "Psychics and prophecies can give you insights to the future, but each individual controls his or her ultimate destiny. Where your future takes you depends on the choices you make. It's up to you."

"Well, I'll just have to make sure that I don't do anything to break Amanda's heart, that's all," Molly said, getting up from the chair. "No big." She would never intentionally hurt her twin sister.

Now she'd have to be extra careful that she didn't do it *unintentionally*.

chapter 2

After Sonia left, the girls joined Amanda in the kitchen. She was removing two steaming pizzas from the oven, one with mushrooms, the other smothered in bright green broccoli and spicy pepperoni.

Wow, I can't believe I made these, Amanda thought to herself, feeling happier. *They look so—professional.*

"That looks *so* good!" Peichi cried. "I can't wait to eat that pizza!"

"Thanks for making these, Amanda," Shawn said kindly. The girls felt a little bad that Amanda had gotten two bad fortunes, and they wanted to be extra nice to her to make her feel better. "I'll run downstairs and get the soda!" The girls had borrowed some money from Shawn's Grandma Ruthie to buy a small fridge, which they kept in the Moores' basement. They used it to keep their supplies separate from the Moores' household food—especially from the twins' seven-year-old brother, Matthew, who *always* seemed to be eating!

"This is the best birthday I've ever had," Natasha told them. "Thanks, you guys. No one's ever done this for me before."

"Is it safe to come back down?" Mrs. Moore called from the top of the stairs.

"I think so," Amanda shouted in reply. "That crazy fortune-teller left."

Mrs. Moore came down, along with Matthew and the family's tiger cat, Kitty. "What's for dinner?" Matthew asked. "I'm *starving*." He grabbed his stomach and pretended to faint from hunger.

"Hmmm, let's see..." Molly said playfully. "There are chips and pretzels, caramel popcorn, birthday cake, and these delicious pizzas, fresh out of the oven. *Mmmm*. Don't they smell *good?* Oh, wait!" she exclaimed, acting surprised. "This food is for the birthday girl *only!* Guess you'll have to eat that leftover meatloaf, Matthew!"

Matthew's jaw dropped. "Aw, no way!" he yelled. "*Mom!*"

"Don't worry, Matthew," Natasha said, smiling. "I'm the birthday girl, and I say you get some pizza. Cool?"

"Cool!" he said, giving her a high-five, his freckled face breaking into a huge grin. Natasha smiled back at him. For the first time in a while, she felt truly, really, completely happy. She remembered how absolutely *unhappy* she'd felt not very long ago. Just two weeks ago, in fact, she'd revealed to her friends that she was adopted. It was something she herself had only learned about a year ago. When her parents had told her, it brought up so many confusing questions. She became filled with envy for other girls who lived with their birth families, whose lives weren't full of secrets and unanswerable questions, and the envy made her feel sick inside.

Finally, Natasha decided to tell her friends the truth. Once the secret was out, it was as if a terrible weight had been lifted off her shoulders. Though she was starting to understand that her *real* parents were the ones who had adopted her, who'd loved and cared for her since she was a baby, Natasha still had questions. But it all seemed less important now that it wasn't a deep, dark secret she was carrying around inside her.

"Thanks, Natasha, that's very sweet," Mrs. Moore said. "But we're going to have dinner with the Baders. Otherwise, Matthew would probably eat all of this pizza himself!"

"You'd better save me some cake!" Matthew said.

"We'll save you one piece of cake," Amanda promised.

After dinner the girls put together a plate of cookies and brownies, a big bowl of chips, and some sodas, and went upstairs to the large room the twins shared. One at a time, each girl went to the bathroom to change into her nightshirt or pajamas. Shawn, Peichi, and Natasha laid out their sleeping bags.

Amanda took out her flowered case filled with nail polishes of all different shades. "Help yourselves," she told her friends. "Here's the clear polish for you, Molly." She giggled. "Since your nails are all chewed up, that would probably be the best."

"I don't want nail polish," Molly protested.

"Use it," insisted Amanda. "It'll help you stop biting your nails, since polish tastes *terrible*. Here, Molls, I'll paint your nails for you."

For the next hour, the girls painted one another's fingers and toes. They giggled and talked about people they knew from school. Shawn told them a scary story about a girl who always wore a scarf around her neck—until her head fell off one day when some kids yanked off her scarf!

"*Ew!* That's disgusting!" Peichi cried with a laugh.

"And it makes no sense," added Natasha. "There's no way that a scarf could hold somebody's head onto their body. Plus, they would be dead if their head wasn't attached!"

"It's not supposed to make *sense*," said Shawn, laughing. "It's just supposed to be scary!"

"*Oooh*, I know a good story," Peichi began.

"No, no more horror stories," pleaded Amanda. "I'll have nightmares. Let's talk about something else."

"I'll read from my new astrology book," suggested Natasha. "Let's see...it says here that a Capricorn—that's me—gets along best with Scorpio, Leo, Aquarius, and Cancer." She looked at all of them, trying to remember their signs. "None of you are those signs," she realized. "Oh, well, I like you all anyway."

"Let me see that book," Peichi requested, taking the book very carefully so she wouldn't smear any of her sparkly blue polish. "I'm Sagittarius, which means I get along with Aries and Leo. So I should get along best with Shawn."

"And we *do* get along," Shawn said.

"True, but I don't get along better with you than with the rest of the group," Peichi pointed out.

"Maybe this stuff just isn't real," Natasha said, feeling her sensible side resurfacing. "I mean, it's fun, but we shouldn't be taking it all that seriously."

"I know what you mean," said Molly. "I don't believe in those predictions, either. I'd never break Amanda's heart."

"You'd better not," Amanda teased. "How could you possibly break my heart? We share *everything*. And we definitely tell each other everything." Still, Amanda couldn't stop thinking about how Sonia seemed to know *exactly* how she was feeling about Shawn.

"What I want to know," Shawn said, "is how Sonia knew that I'm involved with cooking. And she seemed to know that it's just me and my dad."

"This kind of horoscope isn't the only horoscope there is, you know," Peichi said. "The Chinese have a different set of signs based on what year you were born instead of what month."

"That's neat," Natasha said. "We all have the same sign!"

"Well, not exactly," Peichi corrected her. "Amanda, Molly, Shawn, and I have the same sign. But your birthday is January thirteenth—that's before the Chinese New Year happens, Natasha, so your sign is for the year before."

"Oh, *that* figures," Natasha said, rolling her eyes. *Just when I think I'm finally the same as everyone else, I find out I'm still different!* she thought to herself.

"But Peichi, according to the Chinese horoscopes, almost everybody born in the same year would be sort of similar to one another," Molly said. "But Amanda and I were born just minutes apart and we're not that much alike, except for our looks."

Peichi shrugged. "Don't ask me. I'm just telling you what they say. Listen, you guys, Chinese New Year is coming up. It's only two weeks away! I'm so excited! At the end of the holiday, it's a tradition that friends and relatives come over for a big dinner. My parents said that this year I could invite some of *my* friends over! Do you all want to come?" Peichi took a deep breath after talking so fast, and all the girls giggled.

"Absolutely," Amanda said, blowing on her bright red toes to dry them.

"That sounds great," Molly agreed. "But why isn't Chinese New Year celebrated on January first?"

"The traditional Chinese calendar is different from

the western calendar. We don't do all that A.D. and B.C. stuff, which means we count the years differently," Peichi explained.

"I get it," Molly said. "It sounds really cool, Peichi. It's so awesome that last month we went to Natasha's for Hanukkah, and next month we'll be at your house for the Chinese New Year."

"I *love* Chinese food," said Shawn. "Who will be doing the New Year's cooking at your house, Peichi?"

"My whole family! Everyone contributes to the meal. And here's the big thing," Peichi said eagerly. "My parents said that you guys could cook with us, if you want."

"Cool!" Amanda said. "Would we cook at your place or at your grandparents' in Chinatown?"

"I'd love to go to Chinatown," said Natasha. "I've only been there a few times with my parents. Manhattan is so big! Sometimes I get a little nervous there."

"I like it better here in Brooklyn, too," Molly agreed.

"Not me," stated Amanda. "I *love* Manhattan. That's where all the excitement is—the theaters, the TV studios. And all the celebrities! The minute I'm finished with college, I'm getting an apartment in the city."

"Hey, I thought we planned to live together after school," Molly reminded her. "I don't want to live in Manhattan."

"You have to," Amanda said slowly as a sly look came over her face. "If you don't, you'll break my heart."

"Oh, great!" Molly cried, throwing her arms wide. "Now she's going to hold that over my head for the rest of my life so she can get me to do whatever she wants."

Everybody laughed. "No, I won't," insisted Amanda. "We'll flip a coin. Or maybe I'll find some amazing apartment in Manhattan that will convince you to live there!"

"Wouldn't that be so cool?" Shawn asked.

"You can live with us," Amanda said. *As long as you don't bring Angie with you,* she thought.

"I want to live with you guys, too," Peichi said. "And so does Natasha. We could cook gourmet meals and deliver them all over New York City! Amanda could go on auditions in the theater district. Natasha would be at the TV studios in the West Fifties every day since she's going to be a TV star. And Molly, Shawn, and I would go to Yankee Stadium and watch ball games whenever we weren't cooking or delivering food!"

"It sounds great," Molly said. "Maybe we could even have our own restaurant. That would be awesome. I wonder if it will ever really happen."

"We should get Sonia back here to ask her," suggested Shawn.

"I wonder if she believes the things she says or just makes them up," Amanda said. She still couldn't shake the uneasy feeling she had from Sonia's predictions.

"I think it was real," Shawn said. "She seemed to really be concentrating, and she never changed her story or backed down. It was like she saw what she saw, and that was it. If she were only making it up, wouldn't she have given everyone a good fortune that they wanted to hear?"

"I got the only really positive fortune, and I don't even want to be a TV star," Natasha said.

"You don't?" Amanda asked. "I do. I'll take your fortune, then. It beats losing your best friend."

"She only said you'd *feel* like you were losing your best friend," Shawn reminded her. "She didn't say you'd actually *lose* your best friend."

Amanda wondered if Shawn knew that she was the best friend who would be lost. Shawn didn't seem to be worried about it, though. But the more Amanda thought about it, the more certain she became that Shawn was the one Sonia had been referring to.

"Anyway," Peichi said, changing the subject back to Chinese New Year. "Ah-mah said she'd give us a cooking lesson next weekend, if you guys want." Ah-mah was Peichi's grandmother.

"Awesome—another guest chef, just like Grandma Ruthie," Shawn said. A few months ago, Shawn's dad had taken a long business trip to Australia. Shawn's Grandma Ruthie had stayed with her in New York, and she had taught the girls how to cook Southern food, her specialty. The clients loved it!

"*Ohhh!* I almost forgot!" squealed Amanda, reaching

for her backpack. She pulled out lots of little tubes and jars. "I bought this glimmery lotion at the drugstore. And I got some free samples of these cool masks and moisturizers. We can each try a different one!"

"Awesome!" Shawn exclaimed. She, Peichi, and Natasha grabbed the brightly colored tubes and rushed off to the twins' bathroom to try them out. As Shawn left the room, Amanda sighed heavily. She couldn't stop thinking about Sonia's prediction—about losing Shawn.

"Don't worry, Manda," Molly said, putting her hand on Amanda's arm. "You're right, it's all make-believe. And no matter what, you'll never lose *me*."

chapter 3

On Sunday afternoon, Peichi walked home from the sleepover. She yawned. The girls had been up *really* late, talking until four o'clock in the morning, and even though they'd slept in past noon, she still felt tired. As she hiked up the sloping city block, she thought about how much she was looking forward to Chinese New Year. The fact that her parents were treating her like a grown-up—involving her in their plans, letting her invite her friends—made it seem even more special. She couldn't wait to have her friends experience all the fun of Chinese New Year, too. And she couldn't wait to receive *ly-cee*—red envelopes stuffed with money for good luck!

"I'm home!" she called as she walked in the front door of her house.

"So am I," called her slim, stylish mother, coming up the front hall to her. Smiling warmly, she hugged Peichi. "How was the sleepover?"

"It was great! Natasha was completely surprised. And I told everybody about Chinese New Year. They're all really excited about it. They're going to help cook and everything."

"I'm glad," Mrs. Cheng said, putting her arm around

Peichi's shoulders. "I think the holiday will be extra fun this year. Homework?"

"A little."

"Go upstairs and do it now while you're still awake," her mother said. "I'm guessing you'll conk out early tonight."

"I'm not tired," Peichi said. Then she yawned so wide that she realized she must be more tired than she thought. She and her mother both laughed. "I guess I *am* a little tired," she admitted.

"Get that homework done," her mother urged.

Peichi went upstairs to her bedroom. She loved her bedroom, with its ivory chenille rug, sheer ivory drapes, fun pink Lava Lamp, and comfy, aqua leopard-print pillows. Peichi pulled her long, shiny black hair into a ponytail so it wouldn't fall in her face while she worked. She took her social studies book out of her school backpack. Holding it to her chest, she bounced onto her large sleigh bed and opened the book to the assigned chapter: "British Rule in India." The assignment was to read the chapter and answer some questions.

Peichi got out her notebook but instead of starting on the questions, she started doodling and drew the dragon dancers that always led the Chinese New Year parades to the sounds of drums. They danced in front of shops to bring the shops good luck for the new year.

Before I start answering these questions, I'll just make a list of things I need to do to get ready for Chinese New Year, she decided. She pictured the crowd in Chinatown as people gathered to watch dancers performing a dragon dance. People dressed in the large costume of an Asian dragon would perform inside the suit. Exotic Chinese music would blast from speakers mounted on the buildings.

Another image formed in her mind. She was with her friends at a market in Chinatown. Peichi saw herself pointing out the foods they wouldn't be familiar with, like bok choy, litchi nuts, catfish, and dried bean curd. In the picture she was smiling, feeling proud. Her friends were impressed and excited to be there.

From somewhere, Chinese music filled the street. Peichi imagined herself listening to it, being lulled by its sweet sounds...and soon she was sound asleep.

"How was I supposed to know that we'd have a pop quiz on the British rule in India?" Peichi complained to her friends the next day at lunch. "And even if I *had* known, I didn't *mean* to fall asleep. It just kind of *happened*. My parents should have woken me up, but they thought I was exhausted from the party and they wanted me to get my sleep for Monday."

"Did you get *any* of the questions right?" asked Molly.

"I don't know. I just guessed at the answers as best as I could," Peichi said. She stared down at her lunch. Somehow, she wasn't very hungry.

"Hey, guys, ask me what I'm planning to do next month," Molly said, changing the subject.

"What are you going to do?" Shawn asked.

"I'm going to try out for softball," Molly answered.

"Softball? You are?" Natasha questioned. "I didn't know you were interested in softball! When did you decide to try out?"

"The other day when Athena suggested it," Molly told her. In the beginning of the school year, Molly had struggled with math, so she had started getting weekly tutoring from Athena Vardalos, a seventh-grader. "Last night Athena called and asked me if we could switch the regular afternoons when we work together because softball practice is starting in a month and she's on the team. She's been on the team since sixth grade."

"She talked you into trying out?" Shawn asked.

"Well, she suggested it, since she knows I like sports," Molly answered. "It sounds fun. I've always liked to play, but we never had a team in elementary school."

"Molly can really hit the ball," Amanda said. "I just jump back when I see that ball fly at my face!"

"Softball won't interfere with you coming to Chinese New Year, will it, Molly?" Peichi asked. "That's next month, too."

"I don't think so," Molly said. "I don't know what the tryout or practice schedule will be yet, but don't worry. I'll make sure I'm around."

"Good," Peichi said, smiling. "There's so much to do! I've already started making plans."

"Isn't it a little soon to start?" Amanda asked.

"No way! This is a *huge* event in my family. When all my relatives get together, there are fifty of them. Then my parents have, like, a zillion friends who come over, too. My whole house is *packed* with people on that day, wearing red for good luck. It's like a huge party."

"Cool!" said Amanda. She couldn't really imagine Peichi's large house *completely* filled with people.

"So, who wants to come over today?" Peichi asked.

"Sorry," Shawn said, shaking her head. "I have cheer-leading practice. And I have to study for the big English test tomorrow. I love *A Tree Grows in Brooklyn*. I think it's my new favorite book."

"I really liked it, too," Amanda agreed. "But I still need to study my notes. Did you like it, Peichi?"

Peichi shrugged. "I haven't really finished it yet. But the first chapter was pretty good. A little slow, maybe, but good."

Shawn's mouth dropped open. "You haven't finished

it? Peichi, that book is, like, four hundred pages! You'd better stay home and read tonight."

"I took really good notes in class," Peichi retorted. But inside, she knew Shawn was right.

That night, Peichi's copy of *A Tree Grows in Brooklyn* lay open on the bed. She had read up to Chapter Nine. Her notes were spread out over the book. Peichi sighed and looked around her room. *I'm sick of reading,* she thought. *I've been reading for two hours already! I need a little break.*

Slamming the book shut, Peichi went downstairs and turned on the computer. Right now it was really important to get going on plans for Chinese New Year. Everything had to be just right. *Maybe there's something I can do to get the rest of the Chef Girls excited about Chinese New Year,* she thought. *But what?* Peichi logged on to the Internet and typed in the address of a website that featured free e-cards.

Scanning down the list of available cards, she found a card for Chinese New Year. She clicked on it and previewed the card. A small burst of red appeared in the middle of the screen. Yellow streamers began shooting from its center. In the next few seconds, the entire screen looked alive with fireworks. Then the words *Happy New*

Year began scrolling across the bottom of the screen. *Awesome,* Peichi thought, smiling. *That's perfect!*

She typed in her friends' e-mail addresses, then hit SEND.

"Are you ready for bed?" Mr. Cheng asked from the doorway of the den. "It's getting late."

"I'm not ready, but I'll do that now," she replied as she shut down the computer. "Night, Dad." Peichi hugged her father as she went past him on her way out. She ran back up the stairs to her room and read over her notes twice, then packed up her bag. She felt a pang of guilt for not finishing the book. *Oh well, I tried,* she thought as she tried to brush it away. *I read the notes really well. I'm sure the test will focus on the notes. Mrs. Weyn always goes over the important things in class.*

The next day Peichi took her English test. She wasn't sure of some of the answers, but she tried her best to guess at them. She was surprised at how much of the book Mrs. Weyn hadn't talked about in class. As the girls dropped their heavy backpacks on the cafeteria table at lunch, Shawn and Amanda groaned.

"That test was tough!" Shawn said.

"No way," Peichi said. "You probably aced it. You worry too much."

"Easy for you to say," Amanda commented. "You always get straight *As,* Peichi."

But this time, Peichi wasn't so sure.

4

On Tuesday night, Molly and Amanda sat at the kitchen table doing homework. The phone rang and they both jumped up to get it. As always, Amanda managed to grab it first. "Hello? Yes, this is Dish."

Molly watched Amanda's eyes go wide with surprise. Whoever was on the other end was doing a lot of talking. Amanda just kept listening and looking more and more amazed. "How many kids?" she asked at one point. "Wow!"

Molly couldn't take it anymore. "What's going on?" she asked.

Amanda mouthed her reply: *big job!* She listened some more and then finally spoke. "I'm pretty sure we can help you. But I couldn't take a job this large without consulting with my business partners first!"

Way to go, Manda! Molly silently cheered. Last month Amanda had agreed to have Dish cater a big Christmas party for one of their teachers, Brenda Barlow, before she had even asked the rest of the Chef Girls. They'd made her promise not to do that again—and she'd remembered. This was a big step for Amanda, who was trying to be less impulsive and selfish, and to think more about others.

"All right," Amanda continued talking. "I'll get back to you tomorrow. Thanks for thinking of Dish."

"What was that?" Molly wanted to know the moment Amanda hung up the phone. "What was that person saying? You should have seen your face. It was halfway between shock and disbelief."

Amanda sat down, her eyes sparkling excitedly. "We've just been offered a job and it's huge. I mean *huge!* The woman, Mrs. Kramer, is a friend of Ms. Barlow. She was at the Christmas party. She was so impressed with us that she wants us to make some food for her."

"What's so huge about that?" Molly asked. "That's what we do all the time."

"No, listen," Amanda said. "This woman has seven kids!"

"Seven kids!" Molly gasped.

"Mrs. Kramer's sister lives in Kansas City and she's expecting a baby next month. She wants to go be with her sister for five days after the new baby is born, so she's leaving her seven kids with their father, but he's not a very good cook." Amanda giggled. "She told me that one time he tried to make spaghetti for the whole family and forgot that he put the pasta in the boiling water, and he boiled it for almost an hour! She said it was a big pot of mush."

"Gross!" Molly exclaimed. "I guess that's where we come in."

"Exactly," Amanda agreed. "She wants us to cook eight dinners a night for all five nights she's away."

"Can we handle that?" Molly wondered.

"I don't know," Amanda said. "We'd better have an emergency meeting with everyone to figure out if we can take this job. I said I'd get back to her by tomorrow. Let's send an e-mail to everyone right now."

They went to the computer in the den and logged on to the Internet, both of them wiggling into the same chair. Checking their Buddy List, they saw that all the Chef Girls happened to be online. "Excellent!" Amanda said as she began to type.

To: happyface, qtpie490, BrooklynNatasha
From: mooretimes2
Re: BIGGEST JOB EVER!!!

Hi all,
    Big news! Dish just landed a
gigantic cooking job. 8 people x 5
dinners = cooking dinners for 40
people! Can we do it? We think so
but want to hear what you think.
This will happen sometime next month.
We set up a Chef Girls chat room so
come on and let's talk!!! We have

to let the woman know by tomorrow.
If yes, we need to schedule a meeting
ASAP.
    M & A

Amanda hit SEND and opened up the Chef Girls' Chat Room window. Peichi was already there.

happyface: Will this get in the way of Chinese New Year preparations?
mooretimes2: Don't think so but we will b bzzzE.
BrooklynNatasha: We have a week off starting on the monday of president's day, so we will have x-tra time there. When x-actly is this happening?
mooretimes2: Don't know, x-actly. We're waiting for a baby to be born. ☺ That's when the mom is leaving and the rest of the family needs to be fed. Will try to find out more when we call back.
qtpie490: Let's do it. I want $ for new clothes even though Dad says I have enuf and he won't buy me more until spring. ☹
mooretimes2: Peichi? Natasha?
happyface: thumzup
BrooklynNatasha: me2

mooretimes2: yay! Can we meet tomorrow after school?

qtpie490: ☹ cheerleading practice.

happyface: ☹ flute lessons.

BrooklynNatasha: ☹ staff meeting for school paper

moore2times: Thurs?

BrooklynNatasha: OK

qtpie490: OK

happyface: OK

mooretimes2: it's a date. Thurs. right after school. G2G. Big social studies test tomorrow. b-b

happyface: C-ya

BrooklynNatasha: TTFN

qtpie490: L8R

The next day, Molly, Amanda, and Peichi walked home from school together. They took their usual route along the stone wall that bordered Prospect Park, the huge park that sat at the very top of the sloping hill above Park Terrace.

"How did you do on the social studies test?" Amanda asked Peichi. "I think I did okay. I studied hard for it."

Peichi sighed. "I meant to study last night after we got off the Internet, but before I logged off I did a search for Chinese New Year and came up with a ton of sites."

"Did you read every one of them?" Molly asked, laughing.

"Almost," Peichi admitted.

The twins waved good-bye to Peichi as they turned down Taft Street and headed toward their house. "Do you get the feeling Peichi isn't doing so well in school all of a sudden?" Amanda asked.

"I know what you mean," Molly replied. "It's like she's so excited about Chinese New Year that she can't think of anything else."

When the twins got home, Amanda called Mrs. Kramer to let her know that Dish was available for the cooking job.

"Oh, that's fabulous!" Mrs. Kramer exclaimed. "I'm so relieved! You girls are lifesavers! My sister's baby isn't due until February twenty-third, so there's still plenty of time, but I just feel *so* much better about going away now that you girls are signed up! Now, I just want to talk to you a little bit about the menu."

"Okay," said Amanda, grabbing a pen and a piece of paper.

"Three of my kids are very, very picky. Basically, all they'll eat is pasta! So it would be great if you would make a pasta dish every night."

"Pasta every night," Amanda repeated as she wrote it down. "That's pretty easy."

"Of course, that's in addition to the regular dish you'll be making for everyone else," Mrs. Kramer continued. "My husband refuses to even touch pasta anymore, he's so sick of it! But then again, sometimes the other kids decide they want pasta, too, once they see it. And sometimes the pasta kids want the regular meal. So you'd better make regular meals for eight people, and then enough pasta for four people."

"For every night?" Amanda asked.

"Yes, that way there will be enough flexibility for everyone to pick what they want. And I know the left-overs will be eaten right up!" said Mrs. Kramer quickly. "But they won't eat pasta with tomato sauce every night. So it needs to be simple, but varied. You know?"

"Actually, Mrs. Kramer," Amanda began. *This job sounds like* much *more work than we agreed to!* Amanda thought. She knew she had to talk to the other girls about all of this extra work before things got any more out of control! But before she could continue, Mrs. Kramer interrupted her.

"You know, on second thought, the kids might get sick of pasta and want something else. So you'd probably better make some sandwiches, too...yes, let's say three sandwiches for each night. Peanut butter and jelly...that's creamy peanut butter with seedless strawberry jelly. It *has* to be seedless or they won't eat it. On white bread. Oh, and don't forget to cut off the crusts! And cut one of the sandwiches into triangles—that's for my youngest, Mikey. It's fine to cut the other sandwiches into rectangles."

Amanda felt as if her head was spinning as she wrote down all these instructions. "Mrs. Kramer, wait," she finally broke in. "This sounds like a lot more work—"

"Oh, nonsense!" said Mrs. Kramer lightly. "It might sound like a lot, but it's not that bad! After all, I do it every day! You girls will be fantastic. I know every—oh, *no!* Mikey's about to give himself a haircut! Sweetie, put the scissors down *now!* Gotta run, Amanda. Call me if you have any questions!" And with that, she hung up.

Amanda sighed heavily as she put down the phone. *Oh, this is just great!* she thought to herself. *Everyone will flip when they see how much work this is! Why do I always get stuck with the complicated clients?*

The next day, all the Chef Girls met in the Moores' kitchen to start preparing for their big job. "I called last night to tell Mrs. Kramer we'd take the job, and she told me her sister's baby isn't due until the twenty-third of February, so that gives us some time," Amanda told them.

"Excellent—that's after Chinese New Year," Peichi said.

"It's during our winter vacation, too," Natasha added. "That will be perfect. We'll have entire days free to prepare meals."

And we'll need them, too, thought Amanda grimly. She cleared her throat. "Listen, guys," she began. "Things with the menu got a little...complicated when I called Mrs. Kramer back."

"Complicated how?" Shawn asked.

"Well, for starters, we have to make full meals for eight people for each night."

"Right, that's what you told us yesterday," Shawn said.

"But some of the kids will, like, *only* eat pasta. So we also have to make pasta dishes for four people for each night. Just in case some kids want pasta. And it can't be spaghetti with tomato sauce every night—it has to be different pasta dishes. Different, but simple." Amanda looked at her friends. They were all staring at her with wide eyes. "There's one other thing," Amanda finished in a rush. "We also have to make three peanut butter and jelly sandwiches for each day. Creamy peanut butter, seedless strawberry jelly, white bread, crusts cut off, two sandwiches cut into rectangles, one sandwich cut into triangles. That's it, though. That's all she wants."

"That's *all* she wants?" shrieked Shawn. "That's *all?*"

"Amanda, what did you tell her?" exclaimed Peichi. "You told her no, right?"

Amanda bit her lip. "Well, I *tried* to," she said. "But she wouldn't let me! She kept interrupting!"

"Why can't we just make pasta for everybody for every night?" Natasha asked.

"Well, the other kids get tired of pasta. And the dad won't even eat it any more, he's so sick of it," Amanda replied.

"We can't do this," Shawn said flatly. "This woman is crazy! That is, like, *so* much extra work! We have to cancel."

Finally, Molly spoke. "I know it sounds bad, guys, but we can't cancel," she said. "First, it would be bad for business. We could get a bad reputation if we cancel a job this big. Second, I think it sounds worse than it is. Basically, it's the regular job we signed up for— plus a little extra. Simple pasta dishes and peanut butter and jelly sandwiches? We can totally do that!"

"I think Molly's right," Natasha said. "But listen, maybe this should be the last time we cook for Ms. Barlow or any of her friends. They always get *seriously* complicated."

"Yeah, but they pay really well," Peichi pointed out.

"This one will just take some extra planning," Molly said. "Like, we can have some meals frozen ahead of time so we don't fall behind. If we make lasagna, and something else that freezes well, this job will feel more like a regular job when we have to prepare the rest of the meals."

"How much money will we need to buy all these ingredients?" Shawn asked. "We'd better not let the refrigerator get too full between now and then, or we won't have room for it all."

"Right," said Molly. "We'll need to go on a big shopping trip, but not too soon because we don't want the fresh foods to go bad."

"We have to think about what we're going to make, too," Natasha said.

"That's why we're having this meeting," Molly reminded them. They sat together and planned their menu, trying to estimate the expenses. It took more than an hour before they could finally agree on what to serve. The girls were finally—after lots and lots of discussion—able to come up with a menu. Molly wrote it in her notebook.

NIGHT 1. Chicken parmigiana. Garlic bread. Salad with Italian vinaigrette. Brownies. (Pasta dish: lasagna.)

NIGHT 2. Corn chowder. Assorted steamed vegetables. Five-grain bread. Apple crisp. (Pasta dish: tortellini.)

NIGHT 3. Fried chicken. Mashed potatoes and gravy. Broccoli. Chocolate pudding. (Pasta dish: macaroni and cheese.)

NIGHT 4. Lamb stew with couscous. Green salad. Honey bread. Chocolate chip cookies. (Pasta dish: ravioli.)

NIGHT 5. Chicken croquettes with rice. Salad and dressings. Apple crisp. (Pasta dish: spaghetti and meatballs.)

15 PEANUT BUTTER AND JELLY SANDWICHES!!!
(five cut into triangles)

Molly looked down at the menu they'd decided to make and smiled. "I think the Kramers will be really happy with this menu," she said.

Amanda looked over Molly's shoulder and also read it. "Where are we going to get the money to buy the ingredients for all this? Peichi, how's the treasury doing?"

Peichi was the treasurer of Dish. She looked at the list of meals while Molly started another list of ingredients the girls would need to buy. "I don't know, guys," Peichi said slowly. "I'm not sure we have enough in the treasury to pay for this. Does anybody have some money they can chip in?"

"I don't," said Amanda sadly. "I'm totally broke."

"Me, too," said Shawn, scrunching up her nose.

"Uh-oh," said Natasha, looking concerned.

Molly looked up from her list. "Don't worry, guys," she said. "I'll figure something out."

I hope, she thought.

chapter 5

"I love Chinatown!" Amanda said when all the girls went shopping with Peichi's dad and grandmother on Sunday. "It's so exciting."

"Haven't you ever been here before?" Mr. Cheng asked. He was loaded with packages that Ah-mah had filled with all kinds of interesting ingredients like chili bean paste, dried tiger lily buds, and *hua chiao*, a kind of mild peppercorn. Although it didn't look as though Mr. Cheng would be able to carry one more bag, Ah-mah didn't seem ready to stop shopping. The group was waiting for Shawn and Natasha to come out of a gift shop.

"I've been here for dinner with our parents, but I didn't come that time that Molly and Peichi went by themselves!" Amanda replied with a grin. Molly and Peichi smiled sheepishly at each other, remembering the time they'd gone to Chinatown by themselves last summer—and had gotten grounded.

"Look what I bought!" Shawn said as she came out of the store carrying a plain brown bag. She pulled out a sleeveless red silk shirt with a mandarin collar that sat low on the neck with a slit in the center. The shirt had a colorful dragon embroidered across the front.

"Beautiful," Ah-mah said. "The dragon is very powerful, very lucky. And the color red is lucky. At Chinese New Year celebrations, people wear red, write poems on red paper, and give children 'lucky money' in red envelopes."

"That's so cool!" Shawn exclaimed. "Red is a lucky color for people who are Aries, like me."

Ah-mah pointed toward the store that she and Peichi's grandfather, Ah-yeh, owned. "I just need to go in there and get a few more things."

"Don't you have enough? What more could you possibly need?" Mr. Cheng protested, shifting the bags in his arms.

"I need ingredients for *nian gao*. We can't have a New Year's celebration without cakes," Ah-mah insisted.

"Okay. You're right. Let's go," Mr. Cheng agreed wearily. The girls followed them into the store with its many jars and cans of food, packed tightly in narrow aisles. Ah-yeh waved at the girls as he helped a customer.

"What's *nian gao*?" Molly asked Peichi, stumbling over the pronunciation.

"It's New Year's cake. It's very traditional," Peichi explained.

"Peichi, please get some brown candy, glutinous rice flour, red dates, and sesame seeds, the white ones," Ah-mah requested.

Peichi led her friends down the

aisle until she found a stack of plastic bags containing slabs of flat brown sheets stacked on top of one another. "This is really just a kind of sugar that's sold in slabs," she told her friends.

"Could you use regular sugar?" Natasha asked.

"I don't know," Peichi admitted. "But I've never seen anyone try. They always use this stuff." After a hunt around the store for the flour, red dates, and sesame seeds, they brought it all to Ah-mah, who stood by the counter. "Very good. Thank you, Peichi," she said. Finally, they were finished with the shopping.

"Who's hungry?" Mr. Cheng asked as they left the store. "We're on Mott Street, just a half block away from Wo Hop Restaurant."

"Oh, I don't want to walk down all those stairs," Ah-mah said.

"What are you complaining about? I'm the one with all the bags!" he teased.

"Oh, you," Ah-mah said fondly. "Let's go."

Just as Ah-mah had said, Wo Hop's had a long staircase leading to the restaurant, which was below street level. "I know it looks plain," Mr. Cheng said, "but I love their food. I think it's the best Chinese food outside of China—except for what Ah-mah cooks, of course!" Mr. Cheng spoke to the waiters in Chinese and they pushed two tables together so everyone could sit at one table.

The menu they were given was in Chinese, so the girls

needed Ah-mah's help to order. Peichi impressed every-one by ordering a couple of dishes in Chinese.

"Wow!" Molly said. "I've never heard you speak Chinese before. Cool!"

"Thanks," Peichi replied. "It's hard, but Ah-mah helps me a lot!"

Molly noticed a poster on the wall showing a wheel divided into twelve pie pieces. At the end of each of the twelve sections was a picture of an animal. "What's that mean?" she asked.

"Oh! It's the Chinese zodiac I was telling you about," Peichi exclaimed. "It goes around in a circle. Each year is represented by a different animal until it comes back again."

"Does that mean that every twelve years, the same animal comes around?" Natasha asked.

"That's right," Peichi replied.

"Then people who are twelve years apart should have a lot in common," Natasha concluded.

"That's what they say," Peichi told her.

"There is a story about that zodiac," Ah-mah recalled. Because it was easier for her, she started speaking in Chinese as Mr. Cheng translated. "The legend goes back to ancient times. It is said that the great prophet, Buddha, invited all the animals to meet him on Chinese New Year. Only twelve came, so Buddha named a year after each one of them. He announced to everyone that the people born in each animal's year would have some of that animal's personality."

Two waiters arrived, bearing heavy trays of food. "It smells so *good!*" Molly exclaimed.

"Everyone shares," Peichi explained to her friends. "Just take some rice and then help yourself to whatever looks good to you!" There were so many choices—some of the girls' favorite Chinese dishes, like cashew chicken, moo shu pork, and lo mein, as well as dishes they'd never tried before, like shark fin soup, spicy hot bean curd, and sea conch with black bean sauce.

"*Mmmm*, moo shu pork is the best!" Shawn said as she took a warm, thin pankcake, smeared Hoisin sauce on it, and filled it with the shredded pork, bok choy, and mushroom mixture.

"Try the shark fin soup," Ah-mah encouraged the girls. "It has other things besides shark, like pork and chicken. I think you will like it very much!"

"Hey, I'll go for it," said Molly, laughing. "I've never had *shark* before!"

The meal was delicious, and everyone was stuffed when they finally left the restaurant and headed for the subway. Ah-mah and Ah-yeh lived in Chinatown, above their store, but today Ah-mah was coming to Brooklyn to give the girls a cooking lesson.

Mr. Cheng had left his car back in Brooklyn because he said it was impossible to park in Chinatown. Fortunately the subway car they got on wasn't crowded, because their packages took up three seats! Shortly after they started the ride home, the subway came up from its underground path and traveled above ground.

"I'm so glad you invited us to come along, Peichi," Natasha said. "I really had a great time. Thanks, Ah-mah. Thanks, Mr. Cheng."

Ah-mah smiled and nodded.

"You're welcome," Mr. Cheng replied.

Natasha suddenly sat up in her seat. "I just had a great idea! I'm going to write an article on Chinatown for the school paper. With Chinese New Year right around the corner, the timing is perfect!"

"We can help with some of those packages, Mr. Cheng," Molly offered as they got out at their stop. Before he could say anything, each girl had picked up a bag or two.

They all climbed the stairs back up to the sidewalk. "It's snowing!" Peichi exclaimed. She was the first to notice the light powder that had gently started falling while they were on the subway. They walked to the Chengs' house, which wasn't too far away, catching flakes on their tongues and gloves.

"Careful on the steps," Mr. Cheng warned as they climbed the steps of the tall front stoop. "They might have gotten slippery. I'll have to shovel and salt them right away."

"We'll go slowly," Molly promised.

Peichi reached the front door first and unlocked it. "This afternoon we will be making fortune cookies," Ah-mah told them as they went in. "Would you girls like to help me by writing some fortunes?"

"Definitely!" Shawn agreed. "That'll be so fun."

"Sonia already told us our fortunes," Natasha reminded them.

"I didn't like the fortune she gave me all that much," Amanda said. "Maybe I'll change it." Amanda had had fun that day and was happy that Shawn was with them. The idea of losing her as a friend made her too sad.

"Besides, we need to write a *ton* of fortunes for everyone who will come to the party, not just for us," Peichi told her friends.

As the girls hung up their jackets, Peichi went into the den and returned with paper, five fine-tipped permanent markers, and scissors. "Let's go up to my room," she suggested. The girls turned on the radio and settled themselves on Peichi's big velvet cushions and at her desk, and began to write.

You and your best friend will be friends forever, Amanda wrote. She looked at her words. Maybe she really *could* change her fate by writing herself a new one.

You will write something that wins many awards, Natasha wrote. She hoped that by writing this, she wouldn't have to be a TV star. She'd be able to do what she wanted—write great articles for magazines and newspapers.

Molly thought for several moments before she wrote. *You will never break the heart of anyone you love, not even by accident, not even your sister.* Her fortune was so long that she had to write it on the back of the little slip of paper, but writing those words felt good—as if she was replacing Sonia's prediction by making an opposite prediction of her own.

Peichi also thought about Sonia's prediction as she lay on the floor, wondering what to write. Would changes really be coming to her house? The only thing that had changed since Sonia made her prediction was that Peichi had been spending less time on her homework. Peichi tried to ignore the sinking feeling she had whenever she thought about her social studies and English tests. Her parents didn't know about them yet, but what would happen when they found out? Would anything change once they knew? *You will do excellent work in school,* she wrote. Maybe writing it would make it come true.

Shawn liked the fortune Sonia had given her—that she'd always be the apple of her father's eye. Her dad had started dating again just a couple months ago. At first,

Shawn was really upset. But after they'd had a long talk, Shawn knew that she was the most important person in her dad's life. Who else could possibly be the center of his affection, the apple of his eye? No one she could think of. "I can't think of anything to write," she complained.

"Write things you want to happen," Molly suggested.

"Okay," Shawn agreed. What did she want? Then she remembered how much she wished Amanda and Angie would give each other a chance. If the two of them weren't so stubborn, they might start to like each other and get along. *Your two friends will no longer hate each other*, she wrote.

For the next half-hour, the girls continued making up fortunes, writing some for the party guests when they finished writing their own fortunes. When they were done, they cut each prediction into a strip and mixed them up in a wooden box. "Let's bring these down to Ah-mah now," Peichi suggested.

When they got to the kitchen, Ah-mah and Mrs. Cheng were drinking fragrant green tea from tiny porcelain cups.

"Would you girls like some tea?" Mrs. Cheng asked.

"Ah-mah could show us how to read the tea leaves to tell our fortunes," Peichi said with a smile.

"No, thanks! I think I've had enough fortune-telling

for a while!" Amanda said quickly. Everyone laughed.

"Can we make fortune cookies now?" Peichi asked impatiently. "We finished writing our fortunes."

"I'll leave the instruction to Peichi's grandmother," said Mrs. Cheng. She turned to the girls. "You know, fortune cookies aren't actually Chinese—they were invented in Los Angeles! But they are so much fun to make. I think Peichi could make them in her sleep!" She gave Peichi a quick kiss. "Dad and I will be at the Minks' house if you need anything. We'll be back for dinner," she said, and she left the kitchen.

Under Ah-mah's watchful eye, Peichi got out a large glass bowl. While everyone watched, Peichi whisked together two egg whites and some vanilla until the mixture was foamy. Ah-mah preheated the oven to 400 degrees as Molly sifted flour, sugar, and a pinch of salt into the egg mixture, and blended everything together to form a pale, runny batter. Shawn greased a cookie sheet. Then Peichi showed the girls how to pour tablespoons of batter onto the cookie sheet.

"I'm only making five cookies in this first batch—one for each of us," Peichi said. "You have to fold them up when they are still hot, and it can be pretty tricky if you're not used to it." The cookies baked in only five minutes, but Peichi was right—it *was* tricky to fold them into neat little shapes, with the fortunes hidden inside, while they were still hot from the oven. The kitchen was quiet, except for little yelps if the girls touched the cookies too quickly and burned their fingers. But after a few batches, they had the hang of it. It was really fun to hide the fortunes inside and not know who would receive them! Finally, the girls had a tall pile of golden fortune cookies. They smelled great, too!

"Now we are making *jai*," Ah-mah told them as she took out a bag of ingredients that she had purchased that morning in Chinatown. "It is a vegetable dish. Each vegetable has a meaning. Lotus seed is good luck. The ginkgo nut symbolizes silver pieces. Black moss seaweed is for wealth. This dried bean curd also encourages wealth. Bamboo shoots make a wish that everything will be well." She picked up a bag of noodles she'd bought. "See these noodles? We don't cut them, ever! Long noodles symbolize long life, so we never want to cut them short."

"This is all so interesting," Natasha said. She'd been writing Ah-mah's words down in her bright blue notebook. Natasha carried that notebook everywhere in case she got an idea for an article for the school paper. "It's going to make a great article. Ah-mah, how did the Chinese New Year celebrations get started?"

"Chinese New Year is so old that no one knows for sure," Ah-mah told her. "There is a legend about a monster named Nian. An immortal god appeared in the shape of an old man, and he rode Nian away so he could no longer frighten the people of earth. Before he left, though, he told people to put up red paper decorations on their doors and windows to frighten Nian in case he ever sneaked back someday. Nian was scared of the color red. So we always remember how Nian was scared away. We also light firecrackers to frighten off Nian."

"Okay, who wants to toast these sesame seeds in a skillet?" Peichi asked. "We need to get started on the *jai*."

"Um, Manda and I should probably go," Molly said slowly, looking at her watch. "It's almost five o'clock, and I still have homework to do."

Shawn got up from her chair. "That's right. I do, too."

"And we have a math test tomorrow, Peichi," Natasha said. "Ugh." She carefully tucked her notebook into her backpack.

"Oh," Peichi said. "Right." She didn't say much as she walked her friends to the door.

"Do you have homework, too?" her grandmother asked when Peichi returned to the kitchen.

"I'll do it later," Peichi said. "Tell me more stories about Chinese New Year."

chapter 6

Peichi never got around to studying for her math test that night. On Monday, though, she thought she had done pretty well on the test. By Tuesday she received her graded paper and discovered she was wrong. The number 60 was scrawled on the top, along with a note from her teacher that read *What happened here? Please see me after class.*

"Peichi, this isn't like you," Ms. Nelson said. "Is there a problem?"

"I thought I understood it," she said. "But I forgot that the decimal point moved over one."

"Didn't you study your notes?" Ms. Nelson asked.

She hadn't, but she didn't want to come out and tell Ms. Nelson this. "I just didn't get it, I guess," she said.

"I'm here on Wednesday afternoons for extra help. Come see me anytime you don't understand something," Ms. Nelson offered.

"Okay. Thanks," Peichi said. "Do you think I could, uh...take this test over?"

Ms. Nelson smiled gently. "I'm sorry, Peichi, but that wouldn't be fair to the rest of the class."

"I guess not," Peichi said softly.

"I'm going to need that test signed," Ms. Nelson said. "But don't look so upset, Peichi. It's just one test. Come for extra help and I'm sure you'll do better on the next one."

Peichi nodded as she fought back tears. What Ms. Nelson didn't know was that it *wasn't* just one test. Peichi had been getting back bad grades all day. The English exam on *A Tree Grows in Brooklyn* had been a disaster—she'd gotten a D+ and Mrs. Weyn had written on the exam, "Peichi, did you even read the book?" It was *so* embarrassing! And that test had to be signed, too. Her parents would *not* be happy about this.

Her next class was social studies. The teacher, Mr. Degregorio, returned the test he'd given at the end of last week. Mr. Degregorio was really funny. He always joked with the kids. But when he returned Peichi's test, he just put it facedown on her desk and walked away.

Peichi turned the paper over long enough to see an F written on it. Then she turned it facedown again. She was so used to getting good grades that this seemed unreal, as if she were having some kind of school nightmare from which she couldn't wake up.

"Peichi, you failed the pop quiz, and now you've failed this test, which is worth twenty percent of your grade," Mr. Degregorio asked her after class. "What's up?"

"I don't know," she said. Peichi felt so close to tears

that she was afraid if she said anything else, she would start crying right in front of Mr. Degregorio.

Mr. Degregorio sighed. "Well, let me know if you need any extra help, Peichi. I'm always around after school. I'll need you to bring back that test signed by your parents, okay?"

Peichi nodded, and this time she didn't think she could fight back the tears. She grabbed the paper off his desk and hurried to the girls' room. Rushing into an empty stall, she locked it and started to really sob. How could she have allowed herself to get so distracted? Her parents would *flip* when they saw these three tests. When she pictured their disappointed faces, she began to cry even harder.

"Peichi?" Amanda's voice came to her from outside the stall. "Are you okay?"

Peichi opened the door. "Not really," she admitted, wiping her eyes. "How did you know I was in here?"

"I saw your sneakers under the door," Amanda said. "What's wrong?"

"I failed three tests and I have to get them signed."

Amanda sighed. "Ouch! That's bad."

"No kidding, that's bad!" Peichi agreed. "What am I going to do?"

They stood together, not speaking for a minute or so, each of them trying to figure out some solution to this problem. "Maybe it won't be so bad," Amanda said finally.

"Remember when Molly was doing so badly in math a while back? She thought our parents were going to go wild when she brought home some terrible grades, but they didn't. They just saw it as a problem that needed to be solved and with some tutoring from Athena, Molly has improved a lot."

"Yeah, but *your* parents are not *my* parents," Peichi said glumly.

"What are you talking about? Your parents are really nice," Amanda reminded her.

"They're nice, but they expect a lot. I can't bear to tell them about this. They'll be so disappointed in me! Last year I got straight *A*s, remember?"

"Promise them you'll work harder. You *have* been goofing off sometimes lately, right? So all you have to do is tell your parents that you'll work really, *really* hard and bring your grades up and I bet they'll understand."

Peichi blew her nose. "That might work," she said. "I *will* work harder, too. I don't want to disappoint them and I do *not* want to go to summer school this summer."

"Come on, let's go to lunch. You can forget about this for a while. We have gym next and there's no way you can fail a test there."

"Okay," Peichi agreed, "but could you do me one favor?"

"Sure, what?" Amanda agreed as they left the girls' room.

"Don't tell the others about this yet. I mean, I'll tell them, but just not right now. Okay?"

"Okay," Amanda promised.

After dinner that night, the twins checked their e-mail. "Peichi's online," Amanda noticed the moment they brought up their Buddy List. The twins were squeezed into the same chair, but since Amanda was closest to the mouse, she did the typing.

Mooretimes2: Hi, whazzup?

Molly and Amanda sat back and waited for Peichi's reply. "Let me try again," Amanda suggested when no reply appeared.

Mooretimes2: nobody there?????

"Why isn't she answering?" Molly wondered.

"Maybe she's busy doing research on the Internet for school," Amanda suggested. She really hoped so, because that would mean Peichi was taking her school-work seriously again.

"She's probably looking up stuff about Chinese New Year," Molly said. "That's all she ever thinks about lately."

"I think that's all over with now," Amanda said.

"Why?" Molly asked. "Has something happened?"

Amanda bit her lip. It felt strange to keep Peichi's secret from Molly. The twins usually told each other *everything*. *But I'm doing the right thing,* Amanda told herself. *Molly will find out soon enough. It's Peichi's thing to tell her, anyway—not mine.*

Shawn's name appeared on the buddy list, so Amanda sent an IM to her.

mooretimes2: Hi, whazzup?

qtpie490: A lot! Did you see Peichi's e-mail?

mooretimes2: No. Checking. brb

Molly and Amanda switched over to e-mail and found the message from Peichi.

To: mooretimes2, qtpie490, BrooklynNatasha
From: happyface
Re: Really, really sorry

Hi Chef Girls,

    I don't know if you've noticed or not, but lately I haven't been paying a lot of attention to school. Today it caught up with me and I brought home three tests with really bad grades. They had to be signed and my parents took this bad news super seriously. How seriously? For starters, I'm grounded. I can't hang out with you all until my grades come back up. And no Dish. These grades will definitely bring down my average a lot and it could take a while to get my grades up again.

There's even more. My parents aren't sure you guys can come over for Chinese New Year anymore. They said they thought they could treat me like an adult this year but maybe they were wrong. That hurts a lot more than being grounded.

And also, I can't use the phone or the computer until my grades come up. I'm only allowed to use it tonight so I can write this e-mail. After this, you won't be hearing from me online for awhile.

I'm so glad that at least I have to go to school. At least I'll have some way to see all of you. I'm sorry I won't be around to help with Dish jobs and I just hope I'll have my grades straightened out before the big job with Mrs. Kramer. I never wanted to let you guys down, but it looks like I have. ☹

Peichi

"Wow!" Molly said, exhaling. "That's terrible. Poor Peichi. I feel so sorry for her."

"I do, too," Amanda agreed. "You should have seen her this afternoon. She was crying and everything." She turned to see Molly staring at her with a shocked, confused expression. "What?" Amanda asked.

"You knew this afternoon but you didn't tell me?" Molly asked. "I thought we tell each other everything. I told you when I found Natasha's journal, didn't I?"

"I know you did, Molls. And I usually tell you everything, too," Amanda began slowly. "But Peichi asked me not to tell anyone until she was ready for everyone to know. What would you have done, Molly? Broken your promise to Peichi? I *know* you wouldn't have, and I didn't want to, either."

"I guess you're right," Molly admitted. In some ways, she was impressed that Amanda had been able to keep the secret. In other ways, though, it made her feel uneasy. The twins *never* kept secrets from each other and she didn't like the idea of starting now.

"I'm kind of tired," Molly said. "I'm going to bed."

"Okay. Me too. First I'm going to get back to Shawn, though," Amanda said.

Molly nodded and got up from her chair, which nearly sent Amanda sprawling to the ground. "Sorry," she said.

"No problem," Amanda replied. "Molly, you're not mad that I kept Peichi's secret, are you?"

"No, I'm not," Molly answered honestly. "I think you did the right thing."

"Thanks," Amanda said. "I'll see you upstairs."

chapter 7

"Peichi!" Molly called after her friend the next day in school right before homeroom. "Wait up." She hurried down the hall to catch up. "I have to talk to you."

Peichi looked pale and had circles under her eyes. Molly figured that she hadn't slept much the night before.

"Hey," Peichi said. She brightened when she saw Molly. "I'm so glad you're speaking to me! I was afraid you would want to kick me out of Dish after everything!"

"What?" Molly shrieked. "We would never kick you out of Dish. Why would you even *think* that?"

"I was so worried that you guys would feel like I really let you down," Peichi replied. "This is the second time I've gotten myself grounded right when Dish had a *huge* job!"

"Don't worry about it," Molly said with a laugh. "We all get grounded sometimes. Listen, I had an idea. Why don't you come to my tutoring sessions with Athena for help in math?"

Peichi wrapped Molly in a hug. "That sounds great, Molly. Thanks so much!"

"No problem," Molly said.

"Now wish me luck. Mr. Degregorio wants me to come see him during homeroom period."

"What does he want? Do you know?" Molly asked.

Peichi shook her head. "No. But my parents left him a message yesterday asking to speak to him about my grades! They want to have a conference! It's totally embarrassing!"

"Mr. D. is nice," Molly said. "Don't worry about talking to him."

Despite Molly's encouragement, Peichi was worried when she walked into his classroom. Would he think less of her for failing a major test in his class? Peichi liked Mr. D. and wanted him to think of her as a good student.

"Hi, Peichi," he greeted her when she went to his room. "Come in and have a seat. I got the message from your parents and I'm going to call them back. Will anyone be home at lunchtime?"

"My mother will."

"Good. I wanted to talk to you before I spoke to your mother. Peichi, you're one of my brightest students. I've been worried about you, wondering why your grades have suddenly slipped. Could you possibly need an eye exam? It seems as if you haven't been doing the reading assignments. Sometimes a student will stop reading if his or her eyes are strained."

Peichi looked down at the floor as her face turned red. "It's not my eyes," she admitted. "I guess I just got majorly distracted. I really am back on track now and I want to get my grades up as quickly as I can."

"That's great news," Mr. D. said. "I'm happy to hear it."

"I—I was wondering if there was anything I could do for extra credit," Peichi asked hesitantly. "I could do a project or a report or—something."

Mr. D. folded his arms thoughtfully and pushed back in his chair. "I'd have to offer the whole class the same chance or it wouldn't be fair," he said, as if he were thinking aloud. "But you're not the only one who would benefit from a chance to improve his or her grade. Okay! How about this? Write up a paragraph proposing an extra credit project you'd like to work on. Tell me exactly what you'd like to do and when you'll turn it in."

"That sounds great!" Peichi cried.

"Don't start it until I approve it," warned Mr. D. "I'll give you more details in class when I tell the other students about it."

Peichi felt a wave of relief come over her. "Thank you *so* much!" she said. "I really appreciate it, Mr. D."

Mr. D. smiled. "You're welcome, Peichi. Now you'd better get back to homeroom."

"I will. Right away," she said, backing out the door. Peichi nearly skipped back to homeroom. With Molly's tutor to help her in math, and this project to boost her social studies mark, she was going to get back on track.

"What should we make for dinner, Dad?" Shawn asked later that day as she peered into their freezer. "We have chicken cutlets. I could show you how to make chicken piccata. It's a Dish specialty."

"Sounds good," Mr. Jordan agreed.

Shawn took out the pack of chicken cutlets and defrosted it in the microwave. Cooking tonight with her dad had put her in a really good mood. Before Shawn had learned how to cook, they ate a lot of frozen food and takeout. Now, it always made her happy to cook something fresh and delicious with her dad.

Shawn crouched in front of the bottom cabinets that held the pots and pans. Way in back, she spotted the large frying pan she was looking for. With lots of clanging and banging of cookware, she reached in and pulled it to the front. The pan looked *really* old—its surface was covered with scratches, dents, and flaking metal. Maybe another pan would be better.

Setting the first pan aside, she reached in for another, slightly smaller frying pan. "*Ew*," she muttered when she inspected it. This one was in even worse shape than the first one.

"What's the matter?" Mr. Jordan asked, looking up from the tests he was grading at the kitchen table. Shawn's dad was a professor at Brooklyn College.

Shawn rocked back on her heels and stood. "What's

with these gross old pans, Dad? They're, like, a hundred years old."

Her father smiled and took the pot from her hands. "I can tell you exactly how old they are," he said. "They're fifteen years old. Your mother and I got them as a wedding present."

"I suppose I can use one of them for tonight, but we need to replace these," Shawn said. "It's probably not even healthy to cook on these, Dad! What if this surface stuff that's coming off gets in our food?"

"You're right," Mr. Jordan agreed. "I'll scrub this pan down really well and then tomorrow we'll go pick out some new ones."

"Yay!" Shawn cheered. "Now the next question is, do we have capers?"

"Capers?" her dad asked. "Do you mean those little green, round things that come in a jar?"

"Yeah. We have them?"

"No and, to be honest, there's a reason we don't. I can't stand them. I know how to make chicken parmigiana. Could we have that instead? We can put it in a glass

baking dish instead of one of those old pans," he added, laughing.

"Way to go, Dad!" Shawn said. "Dish is going to cook chicken parmigiana for the Kramer cooking job, so it would be great to try it out tonight!"

Their chicken parmigiana was delicious and Shawn decided she'd add it to the Chef Girls' book of recipes at the next meeting. When her father got home from work the next day, Shawn was just getting home from cheering practice. "Are you ready to go pan shopping?" she asked before he even took off his coat.

"Absolutely. Where are we going?" her dad asked.

"Park Terrace Cookware?" Shawn suggested. "They have nice pans."

Shawn and her dad stepped out onto Park Street, into the dusky late afternoon. Despite the freezing wind that blew up the back of her jacket, Shawn felt warm inside. It felt good to go shopping with her dad. He stuck his hands in the pockets of his down jacket and she wrapped her gloved hand around the crook of his arm. They walked down sloping Third Street, past the cozy brownstones to the busy, bustling stores on Seventh Avenue.

A small bell jingled as Mr. Jordan pulled open the glass door of Park Terrace Cookware. "Hello, Shawn," said an attractive woman with red hair who was working behind the counter. It was Carmen Piccolo, who had taught the cooking class the girls took last summer. "How are you?" she asked.

"Fine, thanks," Shawn said. "How are you? I didn't know you worked in the store."

Carmen lowered her voice like she was telling Shawn a secret. "Technically, I don't. But three of the salespeople are out with the flu, and Jim, the owner, is a friend of mine. So I told him I'd help out a few nights this week since he's shorthanded. Is this your dad?"

Her father extended his hand to Carmen. "Will Jordan," he introduced himself.

"Carmen Piccolo. I'm pleased to meet you. You have a great daughter here."

"Thank you. I think she's pretty great, too. She tells me the pots and pans we own should all be thrown away and replaced by new ones."

Carmen put her hand on Shawn's shoulder. "Good girl. You can't make yummy food in crummy pots and pans." She led them over to a large selection of cookware displayed against one entire wall of the store. "This is our best line of cookware. It's what many professional chefs use."

Mr. Jordan picked up a large frying pan and turned it over to read the price sticker. "This costs as much as my first car did," he said with a funny, shocked expression on his face. That made Carmen laugh. "I'm kidding, of course," he said. "But I never expected to pay this much for a pan."

"They're very expensive, it's true," Carmen said. "But we have many other excellent pans."

"We want something just a notch down," he told her.

"I understand completely," Carmen said, walking toward another section of the wall. "These are the pans I use," she said. "They're still somewhat expensive, but I think they're a great value." She turned to Shawn. "This is the cookware we used in class."

"These pans are really great, Dad," she told him. "Everything cooks perfectly because the pots and pans heat up evenly. And the handles don't even get hot."

"Sounds like my kind of pans," Mr. Jordan said.

"You get six pieces of cookware in this one box," Carmen said. "It gives you everything you need."

"Everything I'll ever need in one box?" Mr. Jordan joked. "Now that's a good deal."

Carmen laughed again. "I meant it has everything you need in terms of cookware," she said. "I'm not promising miracles."

Shawn was glad her father was getting along so well with Carmen. Her former cooking teacher was one of her favorite people.

"Now, is there anything else you need? Any special cooking accessories for this budding young chef?" Carmen asked, winking at Shawn.

Shawn turned to her dad. "Well, we could use a couple things..." she said slowly. "I love that mandoline we used in class."

"Mando*what?*" Mr. Jordan asked, making a funny face. Shawn and Carmen laughed.

"A mandoline is a special device that helps you to

carefully julienne, slice, and dice vegetables so they're all the same size," Carmen replied. "And if I remember correctly, Shawn also loved using the microplane zester!"

"Here we go," Mr. Jordan joked, rolling his eyes. An hour later, Carmen rang up their purchases and packed the new cookware and accessories into two shopping bags.

"Thanks for all your help, Carmen," Mr. Jordan said, smiling warmly. "And thanks for teaching Shawn to cook. You must be a great teacher, because everything she makes is delicious!"

"Oh, my pleasure, Will," Carmen replied. "If you two need any more cooking supplies, you know where to find me!"

He really seems happy with the new cookware, Shawn thought as they left. *We got so much great stuff!* "Dad, can I invite my friends to come over and check out the cookware this weekend?" she asked. He didn't answer her. He had a faraway look in his eyes as though he were deep in thought. "Earth to Dad," Shawn said.

He looked at her, startled. "Sorry, Shawn, I was thinking about something." She asked him again about inviting her friends over. "Oh, sure you can. When?"

"This Saturday?"

"No problem," he said. "Carmen is nice, isn't she?"

"Really nice," Shawn agreed.

"Does she live in Park Terrace?"

"I think so," Shawn said. "Why?"

"I was just curious, that's all," he said.

Natasha put down the book she was reading as part of the research for her article on Chinatown. It was hard to concentrate because she just couldn't stop thinking about Peichi. *She must feel so rotten,* Natasha thought, *stuck home alone, feeling bad about her grades, with no friends around to cheer her up.* Suddenly Natasha had a great idea. Getting off her bed, she hurried down to the living room. Natasha picked up the phone receiver and punched in Peichi's number. Mrs. Cheng picked up and Natasha asked for Peichi.

"I'm sorry, Natasha, but Peichi can't come to the phone. She's still grounded."

"I don't really want to chat, Mrs. Cheng," Natasha said. "I called to discuss an extra-credit project with her."

"Oh, well, that's different," Mrs. Cheng said, her voice brightening. "Let me get her for you."

In a minute, Peichi came on the line. "Natasha! Hi! What did you say to my mom? She hasn't let me talk to anyone!"

"I only told her the truth. I had an idea about the extra credit project Mr. D. said you could do. Why don't you do a video report on the history of Chinese New Year? You can talk about which traditions have changed through the years and which ones people still observe."

"That's brilliant," Peichi told her. "This way I can take the subject I *want* to think about and make it work for the project I *have* to think about. Thanks, Natasha! Hey, do *you* want to be in the video? Maybe *I'll* make you a TV star!"

"Thanks, but no thanks, Peichi," Natasha said with a laugh. "See you tomorrow at school."

Peichi hung up and went to find her mother. Mrs. Cheng was sitting on the couch, reading. She sat down beside her mother and told her Natasha's idea.

Mrs. Cheng thought for a moment. "It's perfect for you," she said, putting her book aside. "But you must make sure that it won't interfere with your regular schoolwork."

"I won't let that happen, Mom," Peichi said earnestly. "I don't want to get behind again."

"Good. Now, you'll have to write a really good proposal so that Mr. Degregorio approves it. I think the first step would be for you and I to sit and brainstorm what will be on this video and how long it will be."

"You mean you'll do it with me?" Peichi cried happily.

"I can't film the project for you, but I'll help you plan it," Mrs. Cheng said.

Peichi hugged her mother hard. "Thanks, Mom!"

On Saturday, the girls arrived at Shawn's house, ready to try out her new cookware set. They walked up her front steps, each carrying a bag containing ingredients for the lamb stew with couscous that was on their menu for the big Kramer cooking job. It was something none of them had ever made before, so they thought it would be smart to practice ahead of time.

They were all there, except Peichi. When they walked into Shawn's kitchen, she had the new cookware displayed on the kitchen table. "These are the pans we used in cooking class," she told them. "And we got all these cool little things, too! And new placemats!"

"It's beautiful, all of it!" Molly said. "Look at the Dutch oven. It's so big!"

"Is your dad here?" Natasha asked.

Shawn nodded. "But he's holed up in his office. He's working on a new book." She opened a small box that held her mother's recipes and took out the one for lamb stew. "It says here that the first thing we have to do is marinate the pieces of lamb in orange juice and garlic for at least an hour." They placed the orange juice, minced garlic, and chunks of lamb into a large bowl.

"Now what do we do for an hour?" Amanda asked.

"We can use the time to chop onions, lemon slices, and more garlic," Shawn suggested. "And we can listen to my new CD while we work." The girls began setting out their ingredients and chopping vegetables on cutting boards. Shawn put on her CD player, blasting the music. Soon the girls were dancing around the room.

"An hour is up!" Molly announced when the time had passed. "Dancing is one way to make the time pass quickly," she added with a laugh.

Shawn turned down the music. "The lamb is ready." She checked her recipe card. "Now we brown the meat a little at a time in some olive oil. Then we take the meat out of the pan and add the onion, pine nuts, and spices—saffron, coriander, thyme, and cumin."

They cooked the meat, put it aside, and then added the spices. "Oh, that smells good!" Amanda said, closing her eyes and inhaling the savory smells. After the spices and oil had cooked for five minutes, they stirred in a table-spoon of flour and cooked it for one minute. Then they added raisins and chicken broth, and a pinch of salt and pepper. They put the lamb back in and added chopped tomatoes.

"Now we have to cover it and let it simmer for one hour and fifteen minutes," Shawn told them, checking the recipe card. While it cooked, the girls started cleaning the kitchen.

Mr. Jordan came out of his office. "Girls, that smells terrific!" he said.

"Don't worry, Dad, I'll bring you a plate," Shawn said. "Go back to work!"

"What do we do with these lemons?" Natasha asked.

"We spritz the lemon over the stew just before we eat it," Shawn told her.

"I can't wait," Molly said. "It smells *soooooo* good."

The doorbell rang and the girls looked toward it. "Could it be Peichi?" Molly said hopefully. "Maybe her parents have loosened up."

"Um... I don't think so," Shawn said, looking slightly embarrassed. "I invited Angie over, but she didn't want to cook, so I said she could just come over to eat. I'd better go let her in."

Natasha, Molly, and Amanda looked at one another, shocked. "Is Shawn for real?" Molly asked.

"This is too much," snapped Amanda. Her face had turned bright red. "I can't believe we worked in the kitchen all this time and now Angie is going to just swoop in here on her broomstick and eat our food! That is *so* rude. It's disgusting. I want to tell her exactly what I think of her!"

"I don't know if you should do that, Amanda," warned Natasha.

"Why not?" Amanda demanded. "Doesn't she make you mad?"

"Yeah," Natasha admitted, "but she also makes me nervous. I've heard that she can be really, *really* mean. A girl from her old school is in my math class and she's, like, *scared* of Angie. I'm not kidding! You probably should be careful—you don't want to get on her bad side."

They stopped talking when Shawn walked into the room with Angie. An uncomfortable silence followed as the three girls stood, staring at Angie, who was dressed in an expensive-looking furry purple angora sweater over a long, black velvet skirt and heeled leather boots. Her blond hair was held back loosely with a jeweled scrunchie.

"Amanda, what on earth is all over your clothes?" Angie broke the silence. "Did you *actually* spill that much food on yourself? My two-year-old cousin is neater than that!"

Amanda looked down at her shirt and saw that it was splotched with large yellow grease stains. "I—I must have splashed the chicken broth," she stammered.

"We all get messy while we're cooking," Molly said quickly. "You spill a lot—even when you wear an apron."

Amanda looked at Molly gratefully and then caught Shawn's eye. Amanda's expression said, *See how rotten she is? Can't you get rid of her?* Shawn just looked away, as though she didn't want to be put in the middle of this fight. She went to the kitchen and, using her new potholders, picked up the pot of stew. "We can eat," she said. "I set the table in the dining room."

"Fabulous!" Angie said, heading right for the dining room.

"Fabulous," Amanda mimicked Angie and imitated her wiggly, nose-up walk. The sound of Molly and Natasha giggling made Angie turn around and look at them. Amanda froze, but it was too late—Angie saw Amanda mocking her. She shot Amanda the nastiest look she'd ever seen.

"*Watch it*," Angie hissed to Amanda in a voice so low and harsh that Molly and Natasha could barely hear her.

Whoa, Amanda thought, startled. *Maybe Natasha is right. Maybe I should be careful around Angie.*

In the dining room Angie made sure to sit next to Shawn. "Wasn't cheering practice too hysterical yesterday?" Angie said, angling her chair toward Shawn.

"It was," Shawn agreed. She cleared her throat and tried to change the subject. "What did you all think of the school assembly yesterday?"

"I liked the part about the rain forest," Amanda said. "The tribal dances were cool."

"Oh, that assembly was idiotic! *Soooo* boring." Angie

dismissed the subject. Turning back to Shawn, she began talking about the cheerleading team once again.

"This lamb stew is great," Molly interjected in another attempt to talk about something they could all discuss. But Angie just ignored her. The rest of the dinner involved Molly, Amanda, and Natasha talking together, while Angie spoke only to Shawn on the other side of the table. Amanda could hardly concentrate on what her friends were saying. And she didn't taste the food.

"Shawn, that new movie with Shane West is at the Flatbush Theater. He is *so* cute! Want to go see it?" Angie asked in a loud voice.

Shawn squirmed uncomfortably in her chair. "Would you guys like to go?" she asked, looking down at her plate.

"No!" Amanda said. "Definitely not."

"Yeah, we should probably go home," Molly agreed quickly.

"I'll go with you, too," Natasha agreed, getting up.

"Don't you girls think you should thank Shawn?" Angie said. "After all, Shawn cooked this delicious meal for you. And she did an awesome job...Something wrong, Amanda?" Angie asked snidely.

"I am out of here! Let's go!" Amanda said to Molly and Natasha. She led the way toward the front door. Molly and Natasha rushed after her.

"Wait a minute," called Shawn. She got up to follow them to the door, but Angie grabbed her elbow.

"They're gone!" the girls heard Angie say as they pulled on their jackets by the front door. "That Amanda is such a baby! What a drama queen."

Amanda stopped in her tracks and tried to listen for Shawn's reply. More than anything in the world, Amanda wanted to hear Shawn stick up for her. But all Shawn said was "What time is the movie?" in a low voice.

Amanda slammed the front door as hard as she could, not caring if Mr. Jordan or the neighbors were disturbed. "Shawn has lost her mind!" she shouted as the girls headed down the street. "That's the only explanation I can think of. How can she even stand to be in the same room with Angie?" Amanda felt hot even though it was really cold outside.

"I don't know," Molly admitted. She decided to change the subject. "I wonder if there's anything good on TV tonight. Hey, do you want to rent a movie?"

"Maybe," Amanda said shortly. That's all she said until they dropped off Natasha, then went home. Amanda stomped into the den, slamming the door behind her.

Yipes, Molly thought to herself. *I'll give her a few minutes to cool down.* With a sigh, Molly trudged up the stairs to the twins' room.

Amanda logged on to the Internet and began typing rapidly.

To: qtpie490
From: mooretimes2
Re: ANGIE THE WICKED WITCH!!!!!

What's the matter with you, Shawn? I've
known you a long time and I never knew you
had a terrible mean side. You must have
one or else there is NO WAY you would be
friends with such a nasty jerk like Angie.
My idea of friendship is that friends are
loyal to one another. You always just
stand there and let Angie insult me without saying a word. She insults all of us.
You don't deserve to be our friend if you
let Angie get away with being so rude to
us. You have changed so much and you are
turning out to be as big a creep as Angie,
and it makes me really sad. ☹ But whatever, it's your life, and if you want to
treat your REAL friends this way, you
don't deserve to have us as friends.

Amanda

9

Instead of cooking at Shawn's house on Saturday, Peichi was in Chinatown, standing on the corner of Mott and Canal streets with her mom, dad, Ah-mah, and Ah-yeh. With her parents' video camera raised to her eye, she filmed the Lion Dance parade that was part of the opening celebrations for Chinese New Year. Mr. D. had approved her project and now she was working on it every chance she had.

Even though Peichi had seen the parade many times before, she was still amazed at the colors and sounds around her. A chill went down her spine as she watched men in a long, elaborate gold-and-red lion costume, each holding up a different section of it, dance down the street as they pretended to be the mythical lion. Peichi knew that before it was finished, the parade would wind its way all through the narrow streets of Chinatown and end at Chatham Square in the heart of the neighborhood. The streets were packed with thousands of people. She felt so tiny surrounded by the huge crowd and was glad to have her family nearby. Besides spectators, the sidewalks were crowded with news vans, reporters, and camera crews. In a clearing in the street, Peichi watched the golden lion gracefully dance over upside-down rice bowls. Mr. Cheng held the camera high above his head to capture the entire scene for her video. The shopkeepers presented the lion dancers with elaborate puzzles. If the dancers could solve the puzzle, they were rewarded with money as the shopkeepers bought good luck for their stores for the coming year.

When the parade finally passed out of sight and the crowd began to thin, Peichi turned her lens to Ah-mah and Ah-yeh. Her grandparents spoke in Chinese, and her parents took turns translating their words into English. "Is this what Chinese New Year was like when you lived in China?" she asked, still filming.

Ah-yeh laughed lightly and spoke. "Ah, that was many years ago," Mr. Cheng translated.

"Many, many years," Mrs. Cheng added for Ah-mah. "Here in America the holiday isn't really celebrated for the full fifteen days, the way it was done in China. Here in Chinatown there is more celebration than in the rest of America, but even here it is shorter."

"Can you tell us some of the things people do to celebrate Chinese New Year?" Peichi asked. She knew the answer to this, but she thought it would be more interesting in her movie if her grandparents told it in their own words.

This time Ah-yeh spoke, and Mr. Cheng quickly

translated: "During the Chinese New Year celebrations, there are parades like the one you just saw. When I was a boy, people lit bamboo stalks because they believed the flames would frighten evil spirits. The fireworks that we light during the celebrations are also to frighten away evil with fire."

"One of my favorite parts of Chinese New Year is the lantern festival," Ah-mah said through Mrs. Cheng. "This happens on the last day of the celebration. People hang beautiful lanterns everywhere and they carry them on poles in an evening parade under the light of the full moon. I loved to see that as a child and I love it still. And during the lantern festival there is always a dragon dance. The dragon is a big, colorful puppet that is sometimes one hundred feet long. Young men carry it along on poles as they dance through the streets. The dragon dancers light fireworks, too, to scare away evil spirits from the shop owners, who reward them with *ly-cee*—just like the lion dancers."

Peichi switched off the camera. "Thanks. That was great!"

"You're welcome," her mother said. "Now, are you ready to eat some real Chinese food? Ah-mah's cooking tonight."

"Definitely. Could I film you cooking it?" Peichi asked her grandmother.

Ah-mah shrugged. "Why not?" she asked with a smile. "I always wanted to be a movie star!"

When the girls returned to school on Monday, Amanda was hoping to talk with Shawn at lunch. Amanda had been a little surprised that Shawn hadn't called her on Sunday to apologize, but Amanda figured that Shawn just didn't know what to say. But, to Amanda's surprise, Shawn didn't sit with the Chef Girls at lunch. She didn't say anything to Amanda, and she didn't even look at her. By the end of the day it was clear to everybody that Shawn wasn't speaking to Amanda. She treated Amanda like she was invisible.

This was *not* how Amanda had wanted things to go. In her mind, she thought Shawn would receive her e-mail and suddenly realize how terribly she'd been treating her other friends.

"I can't believe she's not speaking to me," Amanda said sadly on Tuesday afternoon as Molly checked their e-mail.

"Well, she's speaking now," Molly said. "Writing, anyway."

She hurried to the chair and wriggled in beside her sister. "What does she say?"

"Read it yourself," Molly replied.

To: mooretimes2
From: qtpie490
Re: your last message

Amanda,

    You say Angie is insulting but she has
NEVER sent me an e-mail like that! Saying
those terrible things about me is not
something a "real" friend would do. If I
have to choose one friend over another,
I would pick the one who doesn't call me
nasty names. I never knew you could be
so mean, but I'm glad I do now.
    Shawn

Amanda was stunned. She could feel her heart thumping in her chest, and a flush crept over her face. She was surprised when she realized what she was feeling— shame. *That's crazy,* she thought. *Why should I feel ashamed? Everything I wrote to Shawn was true. I can't believe she is trying to twist this around and make me the bad guy!* Amanda tried to take a deep breath, but it caught in her throat. Molly sighed.

Mrs. Moore walked up behind them. "You two look pretty unhappy," she noticed. "Bad news on the Internet?"

"Kind of, yeah," Amanda replied slowly. She explained to Mom what had been happening with Shawn. *Mom will*

know how to fix this, she thought with some relief. "Here's the message I sent her," she said, clicking on Old Mail and bringing up the message.

Mom read it. At first, she said nothing. "That's some message," she finally said. "I guess you were pretty mad."

"Mad is not the word," Molly said. "Furious is more like it."

"There's a rule about writing angry letters," Mom said gently. "Wait three days before mailing them. You can write it and let off steam. But reread it again in three days to make sure you really want to send it, because once it's gone, you can't get it back."

Amanda exhaled sharply. "You know, she says I said terrible things about her, but I didn't. I said terrible things about Angie, which are all *true!*" she cried.

"You implied that she was just the same as Angie," Mom pointed out.

"What am I supposed to do?" Amanda asked. "I can't just stand around and not say how I feel! It really hurts my feelings that Shawn doesn't stop Angie from being so mean to me."

"There are constructive ways to express how you feel," Mrs. Moore said, "and there are ways that are destructive. But if you stick to expressing only how you feel, it's easier to make your point without making things worse."

Molly put her arm around Amanda to comfort her. She wanted to say something helpful, but she couldn't think of anything. Ever since middle school began, she also felt terrible about what was happening with Shawn. For some reason, though, Amanda seemed even more upset by it.

"I know you don't want to hear this, Amanda," Mom continued, "but I'm going to say it anyway. Sometimes people grow apart. This doesn't just happen with kids, it happens to adults, too. It might be time to start pursuing other friendships."

Molly and Amanda looked at each other with surprised expressions. The idea seemed so extreme. Replace Shawn with other friends? Could Mom be serious?

Amanda sighed deeply. "I hate this," she said. "But I guess whatever is going to happen will happen. There's no sense fighting it."

"You sound like Sonia," Molly said, smiling.

"Sonia was the one who said I'd feel like I was losing my best friend," Amanda reminded her. "Boy, was she right." Amanda looked to Mom. "Would you help me write a better message to Shawn?" she requested. "If this friendship is going to end, I don't want to be the one who ended it."

"Sure," Mom agreed. "I'll help you do it right now."

Amanda thought a moment about what Mom had said about forming new friendships. "After we're done with the letter, I'm going to call Tessa, that girl I met when I was in the play last fall. Maybe we can go to a movie next weekend or something."

After about thirty minutes, Mom and Amanda had an e-mail ready to send to Shawn.

To: qtpie490
From: mooretimes2
Re: sorry

Dear Shawn,

    First, I wanna tell you I'm sorry for
sending you that e-mail when I was really,
really mad. I didn't want to hurt your
feelings or anything. But I was so upset
that I just wrote it really fast and
didn't think about making you upset.
Obviously you got upset from my e-mail
and I didn't want that to happen. I
don't think you're mean or nasty.
You're my best friend, Shawn.

    That's why I get so upset about Angie.
She is always saying really mean things
to me—right in front of you. And it hurts
my feelings that you don't stick up for
me or even tell her to stop. I feel like
I'm losing you as my best friend, which
makes me sad.

    Anyway, that's how I feel. I never
meant to hurt your feelings with that

e-mail. I hope you forgive me.

    Your friend (I hope),

    Amanda

"Should I wait three days before sending this?" Amanda asked. "I really don't want to. I want to get things back on track with Shawn as soon as I can."

Mom smiled at her. "Go ahead and send it, honey. I think you did a good job."

"No, *we* did," said Amanda. "Thanks, Mom."

On Saturday afternoon, Molly sat at the kitchen table and stared down at the menu they'd created for their big job for the Kramers. Everything about it was great. There was now only one problem—a really major problem. *Where are we ever gonna get the money to pay for this?* she wondered.

Back when they'd first started Dish, Peichi's mom had talked to them about investing their earnings into the business. That meant they should take some of the money they earned and buy the things they needed to run Dish instead of spending all the money on themselves. This had turned out to be a good idea and, for the most part, they'd calculated how much money they'd need pretty well. But now they had a bigger job than they'd ever had before, and there just wasn't enough money in their treasury to pay for it.

Mr. Moore came into the kitchen with Matthew. He opened the refrigerator and stared into it, running his fingers through his graying black hair. "You girls haven't been cooking lately," he noted. "I don't see the usual selection of wonderful things to snack on in here."

"Yeah, no brownies, no chocolate chip cookies," Matthew added. "What's up with that?"

"We'll be real busy soon," she told them. "Dad, could I talk to you about a little business loan?" She explained to him the situation with the Kramers. "I don't think we should make everything ahead," she said. "We don't have enough room in the freezer to store it all. But we do want to make two meals ahead of time and freeze them. That way, as soon as we get the call that Mrs. Kramer's sister has had the baby, we'll only have three dinners to cook. We'll be under a lot less pressure. And we can pay back the loan completely as soon as we deliver the food to the Kramers."

"I'm impressed, Molly," her dad said. "You're thinking like a real businesswoman."

"Thanks," Molly said. "You know we paid Shawn's Grandma Ruthie back the money she lent us for the refrigerator. We paid her right away out of the first money we made."

"You have good references and a solid business plan,"

he commented. His blue eyes twinkled behind his glasses. "Throw in a free batch of brownies and you've got yourself a loan."

"Thanks, Dad! Oh, and could you drive me down to Choice Foods this afternoon?" He gave her a thumbs-up. Molly smiled at him. "One batch of deep-dish brownies coming up."

She made Matthew and Dad the brownies they wanted. While they were baking, she phoned Natasha. "I was thinking we should begin shopping for the Kramer job," she explained when she got Natasha on the phone. "Do you want to go food shopping with me today? Dad will drive us to the supermarket."

"Is everyone going?" Natasha asked.

"No, I don't think Shawn and Amanda should be together right now. Amanda sent Shawn an e-mail apologizing for the first e-mail she wrote, but Shawn hasn't responded and they're still not talking. Amanda is over at Tessa's, and if we invite Shawn and Amanda's not doing the work, it will make Shawn even madder. And Peichi is still grounded, which leaves just you and me."

"Okay," Natasha agreed. "I'll shop with you."

At Choice Foods, Mr. Moore helped by pushing the cart while Molly and Natasha ran around the large supermarket. Molly didn't mind all the walking. It was all the thinking that started to tire her out. Comparing prices to get the best value, thinking about what they needed for each dish, reading labels, making sure to stay within their budget—it was a lot of work.

"I'm exhausted," she said as Mr. Moore paid for all the food

"I have some bad news for you," Mr. Moore said as the three of them walked out to the car with the food. "The work isn't over yet. Now we have to load it into the trunk of the car, walk it up the stairs into the house, and then put it away."

Natasha and Molly groaned. They'd never before shopped for a food order this large. It took a little more than an hour before all the food was put away.

"I am so tired," Natasha said, throwing herself onto a kitchen chair. "Do you think it's fair that we did all this work ourselves?"

"It's not fair at all, but I guess it's my fault," Molly replied. "We should have waited for the others to help us. I didn't realize it would be so much work."

"I think we should *force* Shawn and Amanda to make up," Natasha said.

"You're right," Molly agreed. If they waited for Shawn and Amanda to make up on their own, it might never happen. She had an idea. "Feel like renting some movies tomorrow?" she asked Natasha.

"Sure, as long as I can finish my homework first. You know how my parents are," Natasha said.

"I was thinking that an afternoon movie marathon would be a good way to get Shawn and Amanda back together," Molly explained. "Movies are always fun, and nobody will have to talk to each other!"

"It's worth a try," Natasha agreed. "Good idea!"

The following day, Molly and Mrs. Moore rented three comedies at the video store and bought a bunch of fun snack foods—popcorn, candy, ice cream. The trip took them a little longer than they expected, though, and when they returned, Molly found Shawn and Amanda sitting quietly in the living room

"Hello," Shawn said to Molly. Just then, Natasha arrived. *Thank goodness*, Molly thought. *I* really *hope this day goes okay.*

At first, things were pretty uncomfortable, but soon the four girls were drinking milkshakes and laughing at the movie.

Molly pinched Natasha's arm lightly. "This is going to work," she whispered excitedly. Natasha nodded, her eyes bright.

Molly settled in to enjoy the movie. Every once in a while she looked over at Shawn and Amanda. They weren't talking to each other, but they were laughing hard. It was a good start. But as the afternoon passed,

Molly found the movies less funny, though the other girls were still cracking up. Her face felt hot, but her hands were freezing. And her throat was getting sore, too. Molly took a sip of her milkshake to try to soothe her throat, but it didn't help. She put the glass on the table and rested her head against the back of the couch. After the last movie ended, Shawn and Natasha got up to go home. Molly walked them to the door with Amanda, but as soon as they closed the door, Molly slumped against the wall, sighing heavily.

"Molls, what's the matter?" Amanda asked.

Molly realized that her body felt incredibly heavy and that her head throbbed dully at her temples. "I think I'm sick," she told Amanda.

"Your face is red," Amanda said, looking worried. She placed her hand on Molly's forehead. "You're hot, too. *Mom!*" she yelled. Mrs. Moore quickly appeared at the top of the stairs. She took one look at Molly and helped her up to bed.

In the twins' room Molly quickly changed into a nightshirt while Mom got the thermometer. Molly pulled back her covers and crawled right into bed. When Mom returned with the thermometer, everyone waited silently to see what Molly's temperature was.

"One-oh-two," Mom said. "No wonder you're feeling so lousy, Molly. Amanda, go get an extra blanket from the hall closet and a glass of water. I'm going to get some

98

medicine." After Molly gulped down the medicine, she fell right asleep.

"She's really sick, isn't she?" Amanda asked Mom as they went downstairs.

Mom nodded, looking very concerned. "Probably just the flu. It's been going around. Fortunately, I can take tomorrow off to take care of her. There's no way she's going to school tomorrow."

After finishing her social studies homework, Amanda decided to go to bed early. She looked at Molly's flushed face as her twin tossed fitfully in her bed. *Ugh,* thought Amanda. *I sure hope I don't get sick, too.*

chapter 10

Amanda went to school on Monday morning, but Mom picked her up by lunchtime—she'd come down with the flu, too.

Peichi arrived at school on Monday excited to see her friends. All weekend she'd worked on her Chinese New Year film and she'd loved every second of it. "I might be a filmmaker when I'm older," she told her parents. "I really like working with the camera." During the past weekend, she'd walked around Chinatown with her parents and filmed the sayings people tacked to their doors and to the fronts of stores. *All your hard work will soon pay off* read one card that was tacked to the front door of an apartment building. Peichi filmed it, then turned the camera to face herself and spoke into it, saying: "I sure hope that one is true for me."

Since being grounded, Peichi had started to really like going to school every day. It was the only time she could be with all her friends. But on Tuesday, she couldn't find anyone. *That's weird,* she thought. *Molly and Amanda are home sick, but where are Shawn and Natasha?*

By lunchtime, Peichi had figured out that Shawn and Natasha had stayed home from school. *Uh-oh,* thought

Peichi. *They must all have the flu! I bet the only reason I'm not sick is because I've been grounded and haven't been hanging out with them.* Peichi walked into the cafeteria all by herself. Even though she had lunch there every day, it suddenly felt overwhelming—large and bright and loud. *Oh no,* she thought suddenly. *Who can I eat lunch with today? I'll feel so lame if I have to eat all by myself!*

Without her friends there, the day seemed to drag on slowly. At lunch, she ended up sitting alone and studying for an English test she would take that afternoon. She'd reviewed her notes carefully the night before, but now she reread the poems and the notes she'd taken in class.

Wednesday after school, Peichi walked to each of her friends' houses to drop off their textbooks and make-up homework. She hoped that at least one of them would be feeling better and be able to talk with her for a few minutes, but they were all still sick in bed.

By Thursday, Peichi missed her friends so much it felt like a physical ache in the middle of her stomach. For a while she wondered if she was getting sick, too. But she decided it was just loneliness. *That's it,* she decided. *The Chef Girls aren't the only people I know in this school.* She scanned the cafeteria, looking for a familiar face. She spotted Athena sitting with a group of seventh-graders and decided to go talk to her.

"Hi, Peichi!" Athena said brightly. "What's up?"

"Not much," Peichi said. "Hey, is this seat taken?"

"No, sit down!" Athena encouraged her. "Peichi, this is Julia, Emily, and Lauren. Everybody, this is Peichi. She's making a really cool video about Chinese New Year."

"That's awesome," said Lauren. "My parents just got this amazing digital video camera, but they won't even let me touch it, practically!"

"Digital cameras are great," Peichi agreed. *This is going really well!* she thought to herself. *I can't believe I ate lunch all by myself for two days when Athena and her friends were right here. It's so cool to be eating with all these seventh-graders!*

Peichi's good day got even better Mrs. Weyn returned her latest English test—this time, Peichi got an A, and Mrs. Weyn wrote on it, "Excellent!" After school, Peichi was in such a great mood that she skipped up the steps to her house. The phone was ringing off the hook, so she ran to get it. "Hello? Is this Peichi Cheng?" asked the woman on the other end.

"Yes."

"Oh, wonderful. My name is Alice Kramer. Barbara Moore gave me your phone number. The thing is, there's been a slight change of plans. My sister had her baby this morning, so I'll need the food delivered on Saturday."

"I thought the baby was due at the end of February," Peichi said, remembering that the big Kramer job wasn't supposed to happen until after Chinese New Year.

"That's right, but obviously no one told the baby this!

I'm flying out to see her tomorrow, which means I'll need the meals delivered this Saturday by six."

"This Saturday?" Peichi squeaked.

"Yes. My husband will pay for them when you get there. Thanks so much. Bye!" Mrs. Kramer clicked off without even waiting for Peichi's good-bye.

Peichi took a deep breath. This was terrible! How was she going to do this by herself? She was only one person—one *grounded* person!

She quickly dialed the Moores' number and Mrs. Moore picked up. "Hi Mrs. Moore, it's Peichi. Can I talk to Amanda and Molly? It's a Dish emergency."

"I'm sure they'd like to talk to you, Peichi, but they can't talk. Really, they can't—both of them have such sore throats that they're completely hoarse! Can I give them a message?"

"Do you think they're well enough to log on to the computer?" she asked.

"Well, I think so, but only for a few minutes. I'll tell them to log on."

"Okay, thank you. Bye," Peichi said. Next she phoned Natasha but her mother said she was too sick to come to the phone. Somehow, Peichi convinced Mrs. Ross to let Natasha go online for a few minutes. After that she called Shawn but got only the answering machine. Peichi figured Shawn was home alone and wasn't getting out of bed to answer the phone. "It's me, Peichi," she barked. "Shawn, get on the computer. I have something important to discuss with everybody *right now.*"

Then Peichi went to the computer and wrote an e-mail telling them about her phone call with Mrs. Kramer. Within ten minutes, all the Chef Girls were online in their chat room. Molly and Amanda were the first to respond to the e-mail with an IM.

mooretimes2: OH NO! We didn't even get 2 make some food in advance!!! ☹

qtpie490: No way we can do this job. We have to cancel.

Mooretimes2: Can't cancel!

happyface: Agree!

qtpie490: Then what????????????????

Moortimes2: dunno

BrooklynNatasha: Could Carmen help us? Freddie?

happyface: Maybe! I could call Omar, Connor, and Justin 2!

mooretimes2: I don't want boys doing this job.

mooretimes2: Don't want Justin in my house when I'm sick. I look awful!

qtpie490: Let me guess. Amanda sent the last IM.

happyface: Get over it, A & M! We have no choice. Not much time.

BrooklynNatasha: g2g. Mom says I am 2 sick 2 be here. ☹ L8R

happyface: g2g 2. Making calls now. Will let you know what happens.

Peichi heard keys turning in the front door lock. She ran to meet her parents at the front door.

"Mom? Dad? I have to talk to you about something," Peichi said as soon as her parents were in the house.

"What is it?" her father asked.

Peichi told them about the call she'd received from Mrs. Kramer and how everyone in Dish had the flu. "I know I'm still grounded until after I turn in my extra credit movie to Mr. D.," she said. "But my grades are improving a lot and Dish has no one besides me to make this food for the Kramers. All I need to do for the extra-credit project is film our big New Year's party for the last scene. The rest is done. I can show you what I have, and if you like it, you can unground me so that I can do this Dish job. Otherwise, we'll be facing a Dish disaster!" she said quickly.

"Yes. Let's see it," her father replied.

Peichi plugged the digital video camera into the computer and showed her movie on the computer monitor. This was the first time she was viewing her own work, and she was just as pleased as her parents were.

"This is really good, Peichi!" her mother said when it was done.

"You know, it really *is* good!" said Peichi. "Yay!"

"Excellent work," her father agreed. "I'm willing to end your grounding, though I expect your grades to come up and stay up."

"They will!" Peichi promised excitedly. "Thank you!"

"But Peichi, you can't possibly do this job all by yourself," her mother said. "What do you plan to do?"

"I'm going to call Carmen and see if she has any suggestions. Can I do that now?"

"Go ahead," her mother said.

Peichi looked up the number of Park Terrace Cookware in the phone book. She hoped that Carmen would be there because Peichi didn't have her home phone number. She was relieved when Carmen's familiar voice answered the phone. "Park Terrace Cookware. How can I help you?"

"Hello, Carmen? It's Peichi Cheng, your old student? I hope you don't mind me calling you but my friends and I have a *huge* problem, and I'm calling to get your advice and maybe your help! It's a Dish emergency!" She went on to explain what was happening. "So we were wondering if maybe you and Freddie could help us pull this job together quickly. I know it's a lot to ask, but we don't know where else to turn. Oh, please! I'm totally desperate!" She gasped for air.

Carmen chuckled. "Stay calm. I'm happy to help and I'm pretty sure Freddie will be, too. Listen, why don't you call Justin, Omar, and Connor, too?"

"Yes! Yes!" Peichi cried. "We had the same idea but we weren't sure if we should ask them."

"I think you should. We're going to need all the help we can get. Where are we going to do this?"

"I'll find out if we can cook at the Moores' house," Peichi replied.

"Okay, call me here tomorrow afternoon and let me know who's on board for this project," Carmen instructed. "I'll phone Freddie and tell him what's going on. And stay calm, Peichi. I once fed one hundred people who were sheltered in a high school cafeteria during a hurricane with only bread, applesauce, four five-pound cans of chicken chow mein, and six boxes of Jell-O to work with. They really liked it, too! If I could do that, we can get through this."

"Thanks, Carmen. Thanks. Thanks. Thanks!"

"No problem. Talk to you tomorrow."

The next step was to contact the boys.

To: cookincon11, funnyomy478, Justmac
From: happyface
Re: Need help big time!

Hi guys,

   Peichi Cheng here. Dish is having sort of a crisis right now. Everyone but me is sick and we have a huge job we have to

deliver by this Saturday. We were hoping
maybe you could help us too. We'd pay you,
of course. Carmen and Freddie will be
helping us with it. Please let me know as
soon as you can if any or all of you can
help us.

Thanks!

Peichi

Within two hours, the boys wrote back.

To: happyface
From: funnyomy478
Re: saving the day

Hey peichi,

You're in luck, cuz I just talked to
connor and justin and we've decided to save
the day for you girls. You can thank us
later. So this is what we want:

1. limo transportation to school for the
month of february

2. free brownies for the rest of the year

3. $500.00 each

That all seems fair. Thanks for thinking
of the Chef Dudes, Peichi.

OMAR

Peichi laughed. Omar was such a goofball. She quickly wrote back.

To: cookincon11, funnyomy478, Justmac
From: happyface
Re: yeah, right

    Yeah, right, Chef Dudes. We will split
    the profit equally. And forget the brownies
    and limos! But thanks so much for helping.
    We couldn't do it without you guys! And I
    NEVER thought I'd say that!
        Peichi
    P.S. Okay, we'll make you guys some
    brownies—one time!

Peichi sat back, hit SEND, and breathed a deep sigh of relief. Maybe, just *maybe*, everything would work out.

chapter 11

The twins sat at the top of the stairs on Saturday morning and listened to the voices downstairs. Their fevers had finally broken and they had a little energy, but they'd come down with harsh, hacking coughs.

"Hello, Mrs. Moore," Carmen said as she came through the front door dragging a large, clanking bag.

"Please call me Barbara," Mom said, reaching to help Carmen with the heavy bag.

"Hello, Barbara," someone else said. "I'm Freddie Gonzalez. Nice to meet you! Hope you're ready for us!"

"Come in!" Mom answered. "What's in the bag, Carmen?"

"Cookware," Carmen answered. "The big, industrial stuff. Hopefully it will make the job go much faster since we won't have to cook everything in two batches."

"It's so nice of you to help the girls," Mom said as she and Freddie helped Carmen carry the bag.

"Oh, it's our pleasure! They're such great girls."

Amanda and Molly shot each other a thumbs-up. But then Molly had a coughing fit and slapped her hand over her mouth to muffle the sound. This set Amanda coughing and both of them ran back to their rooms.

When the coughing had stopped, they flopped down on their beds. "I can't believe Justin is going to be in my very own house and I won't be able to see him," Amanda grumbled.

"The way you look right now, you should be glad he won't see you," Molly teased.

Amanda checked her image in the mirror. "*Ohmygosh!* You're right!" Her greasy hair stood out at odd angles and her skin was blotchy and shiny. There were dark circles under her eyes.

The doorbell rang and then the girls heard voices coming from the front hall. "Peichi's here," Molly reported.

"And I hear boy sounds," Amanda added. "I think I hear Connor and Omar. And Justin! He's here! Oh, why can't we go downstairs? I know!" she exclaimed. "We can listen in on the intercom!" She jumped over to the end of Molly's bed and pressed the intercom button. Both twins listened in.

Down in the kitchen, dishware was banging and utensils were clattering. Peichi felt full of energy and was excited to begin cooking. With Carmen and Freddie there, she no longer felt so nervous. "I'll go downstairs and start bringing up the food," she volunteered.

"We'll help," Omar offered, and he followed Peichi down the basement stairs along with Justin and Connor. They returned with armfuls of food that they dumped out onto the kitchen table.

"I'm going to put you boys in charge of the peanut butter and jelly sandwiches, the salads, and the pasta—except for the lasagna. Freddie will do that," Carmen said as she read over the menu the girls had written out. "Freddie will also make the meatballs. I'll do the lamb stew—that looks the most complicated—and the fried chicken," she continued. "Peichi, you're on the corn chowder, the chicken parmigiana, and the chicken croquettes. And please show Omar how to make the bread. We'll tackle the sides and desserts as soon as the main courses are under control."

"Peichi, think fast!" Omar yelled, tossing her a bag of frozen corn for the chowder.

"*Omarrrrrrr!*" she shrieked. Everyone laughed.

Upstairs, both Amanda and Molly had their ears to the intercom, listening to the laughter. "It's no fair! They're having so much fun," Amanda whispered.

"I know," Molly agreed miserably.

Amanda walked over to her dresser with a determined look on her face. "I'm going down there," she announced. "I'll wash my hands and I won't cough on the food." She grabbed a hairbrush from the dresser and began brushing.

"Do you really want Justin to see you when you're sick?" Molly reminded her as came back into the room.

"I can fix that," Amanda assured her. "All it will take is some hair gel, lip gloss, and Mom's concealer."

When Amanda was finished putting herself together, she dressed in jeans and a pale pink sweater. But when she got to the top of the stairs, her luck ran out.

"Hold it right there, young lady," Mom's voice rang out. "Back to bed, please."

"*Mommmm*," moaned Amanda. "I feel *fine* and I want to help!" The effort of speaking brought on another fit of coughing. Amanda clapped both hands over her mouth as her mother steered her back to the twins' room.

Molly couldn't stand it. "How's it going?" she called down on the intercom as Amanda, sulking, came back into the bedroom and put her pj's back on. Amanda was secretly glad to get back in bed. She felt worse than she'd let on.

Matthew wandered into the kitchen just then. "Are you making cookies?" he asked.

"No Moores in the kitchen," Carmen announced, gently turning him away. "You've all been exposed to the flu and we need to keep this food away from germs. Mr. Kramer does *not* need to be looking after seven kids with the flu while his wife is away!"

Molly's voice came over the intercom again. "How is it going down there?" she repeated.

"Just fine, Molly," Carmen shouted. "Stay where you are."

"Hi, Molly!" Peichi shouted so Molly could hear her.

"Hi, Peichi! Hi, everyone!"

Mrs. Moore's voice was suddenly heard in the background. "You, too. Back to bed."

"They really feel bad about not helping," Peichi said to Carmen.

"I can tell," Carmen said with a laugh. "The best thing they can do is rest and get better for your next job!"

By two o'clock, the corn chowder was simmering on the stove. A loaf of homemade five-grain bread, a French baguette, and a loaf of honey bread were all baking in the Moores' large oven along with the lasagna. The macaroni was finished and the sound of a mixer was whirring as Freddie whipped up his special brownie dough. The boys sat at the kitchen table, tearing up lettuce leaves and tossing them into a big steel bowl.

"Will we be ready with everything by six?" Peichi asked Carmen. Peichi had finished the chicken parmigiana and was starting the chicken croquettes.

"I think so," Carmen said. "Unless something unexpected comes up."

The phone rang and Peichi answered it. "Moore residence."

A scratchy voice croaked on the other end. "It's Shawn. How's it going?"

"Pretty good! I think we're gonna make it. How are you feeling?"

"Lousy!" Shawn replied. "But a lot better than I felt on Tuesday."

"Well, go back to bed and get better already!" Peichi teased. "I miss you guys so much! I can't wait til you're all back at school!"

By five o'clock all the food was packed in four large cardboard boxes. "I double-wrapped the soup so it doesn't spill all over the place," Freddie said.

"Thanks *so* much, everybody! This is totally amazing!" Peichi said sincerely.

"Oh, you're welcome!" Carmen said. "This was great. And thanks to Omar, Connor, and Justin, too. We never could have done it without them."

The boys clasped their hands over their heads and shook them, as if they'd just won a prizefight. "The new cooking champs are...us!" Omar cheered.

Everyone laughed. "Aren't you getting a little carried away?" Molly's voice rang out over the intercom.

"No way!" Connor spoke to Molly over the intercom. The boys began singing, "We are the champions..."

"And modest, too," Molly commented, her voice filled with laughter.

"We are the champions..." the boys kept on.

"What is this, a new boy band, U Stink?" Freddie teased them.

"Aw, man!" they complained.

"Come on, let's take these boxes to the car," Freddie said.

Everyone loaded the trunk of Mrs. Moore's big old gold Cadillac. The kids piled in, with Mrs. Moore at the wheel and Freddie and Carmen following behind in Freddie's car. They arrived at the Kramers' house, a brownstone on a quiet street. Omar and Justin began unloading the trunk as Freddie pulled up behind them. Carmen and Peichi ran up the steps and rang the bell.

A tall man opened the door. His hair stood up wildly and behind him kids yelled, laughed, threw things, and seemed to be having a great, totally wild time. From somewhere in the house, a dog barked.

"Mr. Kramer, we're Dish! Here's your food," Peichi said.

"Oh," he said. "I was hoping you were my wife and you'd decided to come back early! But this is almost as good. Come on in." He held open the door as Omar, Connor, Justin, Freddie, and Mrs. Moore came in, holding boxes of their prepared food.

"Point the way to the kitchen," Freddie replied.

"It's down the hall," Mr. Kramer told them. "Thanks so much."

"All the boxes are marked with the day of the week and each item is marked at to what goes with what. The chicken parmigiana and the lasagna are the two dishes for day one and the Italian bread and green salad are marked with a one, so you know that they all go together," Carmen explained.

"Thanks," Mr. Kramer said. "You guys are lifesavers! It's usually a zoo around here, but with my wife gone it's like a war zone. Whoa, settle down!" he called to four boys who were playing football in the hallway. "Take it outside!" Mr. Kramer pulled out a large envelope. "Here's your payment," he said. "But hang on a minute. I want to give you all a big tip!"

He handed the envelopes to Carmen, but she passed them over to Peichi. "She's one of the owners of the company—we just work for her," Carmen explained.

Peichi felt herself start to blush. Still, she appreciated Carmen's words. "Thanks, Mr. Kramer," she said. "We hope you enjoy your food and Dish appreciates you business. Here are some of our cards so you can pass them on to your friends!"

Everyone piled back into the cars and drove back to the Moores' house. In the car, Peichi opened the envelopes. "Wow!" she said.

"Good news?" Carmen asked from the front seat.

"Yeah. Even after we pay back Mr. Moore for the ingredients and split this up, I think everyone will be very happy!"

"Don't forget that Freddie and I did this as a favor. We don't want any money," Carmen told Peichi.

"That's not fair," Peichi argued.

"Sure it is," Carmen said. "Someday, make a great lunch for Freddie and me, and we'll call it even." Carmen and Freddie headed up the stairs. "But first, we have to finish cleaning up the kitchen."

"We'll do that," Peichi said. "You two have done more than enough. I don't know how we can ever thank you."

"Lunch," Carmen reminded her. "Freddie and I are always available for a great lunch."

"Absolutely," Freddie agreed. Peichi hugged them both. Then she waved good-bye.

Mrs. Moore turned to Peichi. "Normally, I would expect Dish to clean up after itself, but this was an unusual circumstance. You've done enough work for one day!"

"Thank you," Peichi said. "Do you mind if we just stay here a minute and split up the money?"

"Go right ahead," Mrs. Moore said as she headed down the hallway.

"How did we do?" Connor asked as Peichi counted out all the money from the envelope.

"We did really well," she said. She took out money to repay Mr. Moore. "This is for ingredients," she explained. Then she paid each of the boys.

"If you ever need help again, let us know," Omar said enthusiastically.

"Thanks, you guys," Peichi said. "You've been great."

"No problem," Connor said as the boys headed out the door. Peichi was about to walk out right behind them. But she stopped a moment, looking around the quiet house. From down the hall she could hear Mrs. Moore chatting on the kitchen phone.

With a burst of speed, she raced up the front stairs. She just had to tell Amanda and Molly how it had all turned out so well. Peichi found the girls sprawled across their beds reading magazines.

"Peichi!" Molly cried in an excited whisper. "Did Mom say you could come up?"

"Not really," Peichi admitted, shutting the door. She sat at the end of Amanda's bed and told the twins how great Carmen, Freddie, and the boys had been. "Your parents are even doing the cleanup. Everyone's been really helpful."

"Were the guys happy with the money?" Amanda asked.

"They were *extremely* happy," Peichi reported.

"Good," Molly said. "At first I didn't want them here because I didn't want a bunch of boys having to help us girls out, like we couldn't handle it alone. But, you know, that wasn't right. I was just thinking of them as boys—"

"One *very* cute boy," Amanda cut in.

Molly rolled her eyes at her. "As I was saying, I was thinking of them as goof-off boys and not as friends—friends who know how to cook. It's important for Dish to have some backup chefs just for times like these."

"You're a good businesswoman, Molls," Amanda said.

"Thanks," she replied. "Now I just have to work on being a *healthy* businesswoman."

By Tuesday, all the Chef Girls were recovered and back in school.

"I'm so glad you're all back!" Peichi exclaimed. "And guess what! I've got good news—you're all invited to my house for the New Year's Eve party tomorrow night!"

"Your parents said we can come?" asked Natasha.

"Yep. I brought home a couple of really good grades, and they *really* liked what I've done with my extra-credit project, so I'm on their good side again," Peichi replied. "I'll be filming the party for the end of my film, so look good."

"We *always* look good," Shawn said, laughing.

Amanda noticed a red sheet of paper tacked to the cafeteria bulletin board. Getting up from her seat, she went to see what it was about. She returned to the table, practically jumping with excitement.

"What is it?" Molly asked.

"I can't believe we didn't know about this sooner!" Amanda announced. "There's going to be a Valentine's Day dance this very Saturday. This Saturday! I've *got* to go shopping."

"Why would you want to waste your money on a

fancy dress that you probably won't even wear again until next Christmas? And it probably won't fit you by then, anyway!" Molly said.

"We know why she needs a new dress," Natasha said with a smile.

"Justin," the girls sang out.

"Quiet!" Amanda shushed them. "He'll hear you."

Athena stopped by the table. "Hi, girls," she said.

"Athena! Guess what! I got a ninety on my last math test!" Peichi told her. "Those tutoring sessions with you helped *so* much."

"You go, Peichi!" Athena cheered. "Molly, I just wanted to remind you that tryouts for the softball team are next Monday in the field behind the gym. Are you still thinking of trying out?"

"Yeah," Molly said. "I'll be there. Thanks."

"Bye," Athena said, waving to the girls.

"Athena is awesome," Peichi commented.

"She is," Molly agreed.

When the twins got home from school that day, they were surprised to find both of their parents at home—and in bed.

"Oh, *no!*" Amanda cried. "We gave you the flu!"

"I'm sorry, Mom and Dad," Molly said.

Mrs. Moore smiled weakly. "That's okay, sweetheart," she said in a raspy voice. "You get used to it when you're a parent."

"Is there anything we can get you?" Molly asked, concerned.

Mr. Moore opened one eye. "Orange juice?" he croaked.

"I'm on it," Amanda said, dashing out the door.

"I'd love some chicken soup," Mrs. Moore told Molly. "Do you think you girls could make some?"

"No problem," Molly replied. "Amanda and I will do the cooking and take care of Matthew while you guys are sick!"

When Molly, Amanda, Shawn, and Natasha arrived at Peichi's house on Wednesday night, they didn't know quite what to expect. Mrs. Cheng greeted the girls at the front door, wearing a beautiful red silk dress. "Come in, girls. Happy New Year!"

"Happy New Year!" they replied all together. All the girls were wearing red. Shawn had on the red silk blouse she had bought in Chinatown, and it looked great against her coffee-colored skin.

"Shawn, I love that blouse so much!" Amanda said when Shawn took off her coat.

"Thanks," Shawn replied. "Red is *definitely* a good color for Aries!" Shawn smiled warmly at Amanda.

There were nearly fifty people in the Cheng's living room already. The house was full of live, blooming plants—pussy willows, plum blossoms, and narcissus, which smelled *wonderful.* Ah-mah and Ah-yeh waved to the girls. They were seated in comfortable chairs, talking to a group of their relatives and friends.

"There's Peichi," Natasha said, pointing. Peichi was wandering through the crowd, filming everything from the buffet table to her grandparents.

As the girls approached, Peichi turned the camera on them. "You don't have to be Chinese to love Chinese New Year," she said for the benefit of her film.

"That's for sure," Shawn said. "This is great!"

"Peichi, that dress is *awesome!*" Natasha exclaimed. Peichi's dress was also red.

"Thanks!" Peichi said. Smiling, she handed Shawn the camera and twirled around. Speaking into the camera, Peichi said, "Everything I'm wearing tonight is new—even my headband! It's a tradition that everyone wear new clothes for Chinese New Year."

"So, when can we eat?" Molly asked. Everyone laughed.

"Go right ahead!" Peichi said, taking back the camera and focusing it on a long buffet table. As the girls helped themselves to the buffet, Peichi explained what each dish was. "These dumplings are called *jaotze*," she said. "They're filled with Chinese cabbage and pork. These cakes are *nian gao*. The full name for them is *nian nian gao sun*, which means 'be prosperous and successful.' I hope this video report makes me prosperous and successful!" Peichi joked. "Over here we have lobster and l-o-n-g noodles." Then she pointed the camera at an impressive pile of fruit at one end of the table.

"Tangerines and pomegranates are also good omens for the Chinese New Year," Peichi continued, "and so is lotus root." She moved to a side table, and the girls followed her. "*This*," Peichi said proudly, "is the candy tray—officially known as The Tray of Togetherness. All of the candy on it—candied melon, litchi nut, kumquat, coconut, and peanuts—has a special meaning. And they're all really yummy, too! We also have sesame cookie nuggets, which are *sooo* good!" She turned off the camera.

"Peichi," Shawn said, "these dumplings are best I've ever had!"

"Thanks!" said Peichi. "Ah-mah was in the kitchen all day cooking! My dad even stayed home from work to help her. I love *jaotze* too."

All of the girls went back for second helpings. With all of the laughter, delicious food, and fun traditions, the night flew by. All too soon, it was time for the girls to go home.

"I wish it wasn't a school night," Natasha grumbled. "Then we could have stayed longer."

"I wish that, too!" Peichi said as she helped her friends get their coats.

"Will you be up super-late tonight, Peichi?" Amanda asked.

"Oh, *definitely!*" Peichi exclaimed. "Who could sleep when there's a great party going on right downstairs? Besides, it's tradition that kids get to stay up late on Chinese New Year! Also, I have to get the last shots for my video. Thanks so much for coming, guys! See you tomorrow!"

"Bye Peichi!" chorused all of the girls. As Peichi waved at them from the doorway, Amanda and Molly both thought that they'd never seen her look happier.

But the next day at school, Amanda noticed that Peichi seemed down. She hoped that Peichi was just tired from the night before, but she didn't like the red look of her face or the way she seemed unable to smile at anything. Sure enough, just before lunch, Peichi went to the see the school nurse, who quickly called Mrs. Cheng to come pick her up.

"She shouldn't have snuck up to our room to visit us last Saturday," Molly said.

"Poor Peichi!" Amanda said. "First she was grounded, now she's sick."

On Friday evening Amanda convinced her mother, who was feeling much better, to take her dress shopping down on Seventh Avenue. They went to three shops before they found the perfect crimson dress that had gracefully flowing short sleeves and ended about two inches above her knee.

"It's perfect—not super fancy but really pretty," Amanda described the dress to Molly as she carefully hung it in the closet. "I can't wait for this dance!"

"I can," Molly grumbled.

Ignoring Molly's lack of enthusiasm about the dance, Amanda said, "Listen, Molly, do you think we should invite Shawn over to get ready for the dance with us tomorrow afternoon?"

"That's good idea, Manda," Molly replied. "Is Natasha going? Cause if she is, we should invite her, too."

"No, her parents said she's too young to go to a dance at night."

Amanda called Shawn and she agreed to come over on Saturday around four o'clock. Molly opened the door for her. "What smells so good?" Shawn asked, putting down the large flowered tote she was carrying.

"Nachos and homemade salsa," Molly reported. "Amanda is in the kitchen taking them out of the oven now."

"Yummm-eeee," Shawn said as she and Molly went down to the kitchen.

"Hi," Amanda greeted them. "I hope you're hungry. I made some lemonade, too. And brownies with mint frosting! I'm totally feeling in a party mood. Like this is a pre-dance get-ready party! It's sort of like a sleepover in the afternoon. But without the sleeping."

"You're right," Shawn said, finding paper cups in the pantry. "Not that we do much sleeping at our sleepovers!" The girls laughed and went up to the twins' bedroom.

"It's such a bummer that Natasha and Peichi aren't here," Molly commented.

"I know," Amanda agreed. "Poor Peichi! I still feel bad about giving her the flu."

"And poor Natasha," Shawn added. "We need to work on her parents more! Maybe Amanda can make some more mandelbrodt for Mr. Ross!" The girls laughed, remembering how much Mr. Ross had *loved* the mandelbrodt Amanda had brought to the Rosses' house at Hanukkah. Shawn hung her dress on a hook behind the bedroom door.

"That's adorable!" Amanda told Shawn when she saw her dress. Shawn's dress was straight and short with dark purple swirls on a blue background. "It really goes with your purple glasses. And you won't be dressed in red or pink like everyone else there." She giggled. "Or like me!"

Shawn held up a small bottle of shimmery blue nail polish. "And the dress goes *exactly* with this. Look, it's a perfect match!"

After they finished the nachos, Shawn painted Amanda's fingers with sparkly silver polish. Amanda returned the favor, using the shiny blue on Shawn.

Molly sprawled out on her bed, resting her chin on her hands. She ate, chatted, and watched as Shawn helped Amanda set her hair with Mrs. Moore's curlers. Then Shawn and Amanda shared the mirror as they applied just the lightest amount of blush and tinted lip gloss. Amanda was having such a good time that she let herself hope that everything was back to the way it used it be. *This is like the old days, before Angie came along,* Amanda thought. *Maybe Sonia was right—maybe you really can create your own future.*

"Want some?" Amanda offered Molly holding up a tube of pale pink gloss.

"Thanks, I'll pass," Molly answered. "That stuff makes my lips feel slimy."

"Okay," Amanda said, rolling her eyes. "What are you wearing?"

"My red angora sweater, black jeans, and boots. Is that okay?"

"For you, that's getting dressed up," Shawn teased.

Amanda looked at Shawn, and Shawn nodded. *What's up?* Molly wondered, looking at her twin suspiciously. Shawn shut the door.

"What are you guys doing?" Molly asked as Amanda and Shawn approached her.

"Now, Molly," Amanda began importantly. "You don't have to get totally dressed up. But it *is* the Valentine's Day dance. On *Valentine's Day*. You *have* to look nicer than you would on any ordinary day. Right, Shawn?"

"Right," Shawn agreed, nodding her head. Together, Shawn and Amanda dragged Molly over to the curling iron.

"Oh, come on," Molly whined. But it was too late. Shawn and Amanda were already at work— Shawn adding a bit of blush to Molly's cheeks, Amanda curling the ends of her hair. When they were finished, Molly dressed quickly. She hated to admit it, but the loose ponytail Amanda had carefully arranged her hair in *did* look nice—though she still thought the blush looked dumb. She rubbed it off when Amanda and Shawn weren't looking. Soon all the girls were downstairs, putting on their coats. The phone rang and, as usual, Amanda grabbed it first. It was Natasha. "My parents said I could go!" she shouted excitedly.

"Great!" Amanda squealed. "Do you need a ride?"

"No, thanks. They have to drop me off and pick me up themselves, that's part of the agreement. But I'll see you there!"

Amanda returned with the good news.

"Awesome!" Molly cheered.

"This dance is so exciting," Amanda said with a little shiver. "I just have the feeling that something really *wonderful* is going to happen tonight."

chapter 13

"I can't believe this is the gym," Shawn said as the girls walked into the beautifully decorated dance. Red and white streamers hung from the ceilings. The lights had been dimmed and a disco ball hanging in the middle of the room sent little circles of light dancing over everything. The tables were covered in either red, white, or pink paper tablecloths. A DJ in the far corner by the locker rooms played loud, pulsing rock music.

"Look at this place!" Molly said with a laugh. "All the boys are on one side of the gym, and all the girls are on the other."

"Look, there's Natasha," Amanda said. "She's over by the food table. She looks so cute tonight!"

"I can't believe I'm here," Natasha said when they joined her. "Ever since Amanda gave my dad that home-made mandelbrodt at Hanukkah, he thinks you guys are the greatest and that if you're all doing something, it must be okay!" Shawn and Amanda looked at each other and laughed.

"Well, he has excellent taste," Amanda joked. "You look pretty."

"Thanks." Natasha grabbed Amanda's wrist. "There's Justin."

"Go thank him for helping us cook last week," Shawn suggested. "That's a perfect excuse to talk to him."

With a nod, Amanda walked quickly over to Justin, who stood alone by the beverage area. "Hi, Justin. I wanted to say thanks for helping us last week. I felt so bad that I was sick and couldn't cook."

"Hey, it's cool. I was glad to help," he replied. A slow song came up. Amanda looked up into his face, waiting for him to ask her to dance. She felt *certain* he was just about to!

"I have to go talk to that guy over there about Monday's English assignment," he said instead. "See ya around. And if you need me for any more cooking jobs, let me know. Bye."

He walked away, leaving Amanda feeling completely let down. When she returned to Molly and Natasha, Shawn wasn't there. "Did someone ask her to dance?" she asked.

"No, she's over there talking to Angie, Stephanie, and Jen from the cheerleading team," Molly told her as she pointed across the cafeteria.

"That's the last we'll see of her tonight," Amanda grumbled, feeling her good mood fading fast.

Connor came up to join them and, for once, he wasn't with Omar. "Hi," he said. "Um...Natasha, feel like dancing?"

The three girls exchanged quick, darting glances. Who knew that *Connor* had a crush on *Natasha?* They had been totally clueless!

Oh, no! Don't blush, Amanda thought as Natasha turned bright red. *That's not cool.*

"Okay," Natasha agreed. She'd never been asked to dance before. The song was fast, which made it all easier. If it had been a slow song, she didn't know *what* she would have done!

The twins tried not to watch while Natasha and Connor danced. As soon as the song ended, Natasha thanked Connor and scurried back to Molly and Amanda. She was still blushing, but she had a big, goofy smile on her face.

"*Ohmygosh! Connor* asked you to *dance!*" Amanda whispered excitedly to Natasha.

Natasha giggled. "I *know!* Isn't that so funny? I'm, like, totally shocked!" She took a deep breath. "*Whew!* That made me really nervous. I'm kind of glad it's over!"

Amanda kept hoping that Justin would ask her to dance for the next slow song, but as the night passed, her hope started to fade. "This dance isn't turning out the way I'd hoped," Amanda said softly as they stood against the wall. "Shawn's off with those cheerleaders again. Justin hasn't asked me to dance even once, and the dance is nearly over."

"And this music stinks," Molly grumbled. "Even if you *wanted* to dance, it's hard to dance to!"

Suddenly Tessa bounded up to Amanda. "*Ohmygosh*, Amanda!" she squealed. "*Please* come with me to the bathroom. I have *got* to tell you something."

Amanda looked at Molly and Natasha. "Wanna come?" she said.

"Sure," Natasha replied, standing up.

"That's okay," Molly said. "I'll wait here." Checking her watch, Molly swallowed back a yawn. *At least this boring dance will probably be over soon*, she thought. Natasha and Amanda followed Tessa off toward the girls' room. Molly kept watching the dancing.

"Hey, Molly." She turned and found Justin standing beside her.

"Hey, Justin," she replied. "Thanks for helping last week. Are you having fun?"

"Uh, not exactly," he said. "You look like you're having just about as much fun as I'm having."

That made her smile. "What, you mean you're not loving this?"

"It's so dumb," he commented. "Whoever heard of a holiday about being in love? Every year it comes along and ruins my birthday."

"Your birthday is on Valentine's Day? That's funny," Molly said.

"I don't think so. I think it's pretty lame. But, you know, whatever," he replied.

Molly laughed, understanding how he felt. "So how's the paper going?"

"Pretty good. This spring... I'm getting better at taking pictures. ...ng I want to cover a lot of the school sports—baseball, track and field, all of that."

"I like sports a lot," Molly said. "On Monday I'm going to try out for the girls' softball team. That's one good thing about being in middle school. At least there are some teams for girls."

"That's great," he said. "You should definitely try out." Justin began talking about baseball, comparing the Yankees to the Mets. Then Molly noticed Amanda coming out of the girls' room with Tessa and Natasha. She suddenly felt guilty for sitting there having such a great conversation with Justin when all Amanda wanted from this evening was for Justin to pay attention to her. Molly felt very uneasy. But she couldn't just run away from him.

"Justin, do you want to dance with Amanda?" she blurted out.

Justin looked confused. "Um...sure, I guess."

Still wearing his bewildered expression, Justin walked over to Amanda and asked her to dance. As he spoke, a fast dance ended and a slow one began. Soon the two were swaying to the music together. Amanda looked over Justin's shoulder at Molly and her eyes sparkled happily.

After the dance, Justin smiled at Amanda and said, "Thanks for the dance." He walked back over to the big clump of boys standing around the food, ending with

Amanda joined Molly and Natasha, explo with excitement. "Did you see that? He finally asked me!"

"Yay, Manda!" squealed Natasha.

"That's so great!" Molly said. She wasn't about to tell her twin that it had been her idea. Amanda was so happy, and she didn't want to do anything to spoil it.

"I saw you two talking," Amanda went on. "What did you talk about? Was he asking about me?"

"No, we mostly talked about sports," Molly replied.

"Sports?" Amanda asked, sounding surprised. "Oh. Anyway, I was starting to think I didn't have a chance with him, that he thought of me as just, you know, a friend. But now that he asked me to dance, that changes *everything*. He *does* like me, after all!"

For the rest of the night, Amanda couldn't stop smiling, not after the dance had ended, not while she told Mom all about dancing with Justin, not even while she brushed her teeth. As she drifted off to sleep, she thought to herself, *I knew this dance was going to be amazing. First everything works out with Shawn, and now Justin! This is the best day of sixth grade yet.*

136

Molly leaned over with her hands on her knees, trying to catch her breath. Softball tryouts had just ended, and she'd spent the last two hours fielding balls, batting, and running. Her first time at bat she'd struck out, which was majorly embarrassing, but she had hit the ball every time after that. *I hope I make the team*, she thought to herself as she took a drink of water from the bottle she'd brought to the tryouts. She hadn't realized before how much it meant to her. Just then, the coach posted the new team roster. *Ugh*, Molly thought. *I almost don't want to go check! What if my name's not there? I wish Amanda were here to look with me.*

Just then, Athena raced over to Molly and thumped her on the back happily. "You made it! Way to go, Molly!"

"Awesome!" Molly cheered.

"Practices will begin in two weeks, on Mondays and Wednesdays after school," the couch announced. "See you then."

Molly walked home with Athena. "We could do tutoring sessions on Tuesdays and Thursdays," Athena suggested. "I'm so glad you made it. You're a great batter and with practice, you'll be even better."

Molly smiled at Athena. During their tutoring sessions, she'd started to feel that they could become friends. Now that they would be on the same team, maybe it really would happen. When they got to Taft Street, Molly waved and hurried across the street. She began to run toward her house, excited to tell everyone the great news. When she was inside her house she called out, "Hey, everybody, I'm home. I have big news!"

Amanda rushed down the stairs. "You made the team!" she shrieked.

"Yes!" Molly shouted.

Amanda hugged her and together they did a victory dance in the hallway, hopping in circles and cheering.

"I have some good news, too," Amanda said. "Justin sent me an e-mail!"

"Really?" Molly asked.

"I'll show you," Amanda said. "I printed it out." She pulled a folded paper from her pocket and handed it to Molly.

To: mooretimes2
From: Justmac
Re: Hi

```
     I had fun cooking that day you were
sick. Call me again if you ever need
another fill-in chef. Molly, good luck
```

at softball tryouts today. I know you'll
make it. I'll probably go to some of the
games to take pictures for the paper.
     Justin

"Isn't that great?" Amanda asked. "He wants me to call him to be a fill-in chef. It's just an excuse to get me to call him. Don't you think so?"

"Could be," Molly answered. She didn't mention to Amanda that Justin had written the e-mail to *both* of them—not just Amanda. *Why bum her out when she's so excited?* Molly thought.

"And don't you think that hint he dropped about the softball games is cute?" Amanda added. "He's letting me know that he'll be there because he figures I'll be there, too, watching your games." Amanda closed her eyes, imagining sitting with Justin at Molly's games, borrowing his jacket when it was windy or cold...

Oh, boy, Molly thought. *Did I create a monster when I asked him to dance with her?*

"We also got an e-mail from Peichi," Amanda continued. "She's feeling much better and will be back at school tomorrow. And guess what? Her mom dropped off her video for Mr. D. last week. He called Peichi at home today to tell her how great it was! He really loved it and she's getting an A! So she's officially not grounded anymore!"

"That's great!" Molly exclaimed. "I'm so happy for Peichi."

"Yeah, me too. She's having a big premiere on Friday night so we can all watch her video. Ah-mah and Ah-yeh are coming and everything. Oh, and guess what else? There's a message on the machine for another Dish job!"

Mrs. Moore came in the front door. She'd been back at work again, now that she was over the flu. "I have great news, girls," she announced. "They just told me at work today that they're sending me to New Orleans next month for a conference. So we're all going to go. We'll have a family vacation in New Orleans!"

"New Orleans!" the girls shouted at the same time. "Cool!"

"That's where Daddy and I went on our honeymoon, you know," continued Mrs. Moore. "New Orleans is a great city. We'll probably take a swamp tour and see alligators, and eat all kinds of delicious Cajun food. It's going to be so much fun!"

"*Ooh*, Molls, let's go look at the pictures from Mom and Dad's honeymoon!" Amanda said excitedly as she rushed off to find the photo album

Molly smiled as she followed Amanda into the living room. *Looks like everything's back to normal,* she thought. *Peichi's not grounded any more, that huge cooking job is done, everyone's over the flu, and*

Amanda and Shawn are friends again! But Molly knew that things wouldn't stay quiet for long. More Dish jobs, softball practices and games, and a trip to New Orleans...Molly was certain that her future would be really busy—and really fun!

The Amazing Cookbook

By

The CHEF Girls

AMANDA!

Molly!

Peichi ☺

shawn!

Natasha!

Amanda's Awesome
Brownies with Mint Frosting

THE BROWNIE RECIPE IS ACTUALLY MY MOM'S, BUT I MADE UP THE

FROSTING! IT'S A YUMMY BUTTERCREAM FROSTING (MY FAVORITE!)

WITH PEPPERMINT ADDED!

BROWNIES:

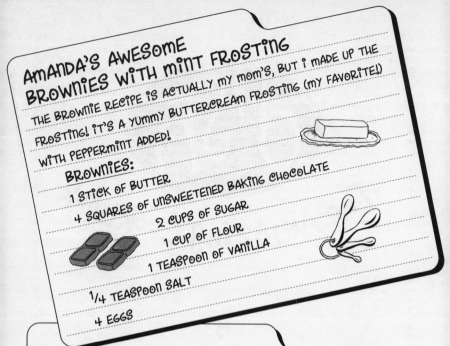

1 STICK OF BUTTER

4 SQUARES OF UNSWEETENED BAKING CHOCOLATE

2 CUPS OF SUGAR

1 CUP OF FLOUR

1 TEASPOON OF VANILLA

1/4 TEASPOON SALT

4 EGGS

PREHEAT THE OVEN TO 375 DEGREES AND GREASE A BAKING

PAN (WE USUALLY USE A 9 X 13 INCH PAN, BUT YOU CAN USE A

DIFFERENT SIZE IF YOU WANT).

MELT THE BUTTER, CHOCOLATE, AND

SUGAR IN A SMALL POT OVER LOW HEAT.

WHEN THE SUGAR AND CHOCOLATE ARE ALL DIS-

SOLVED INTO THE BUTTER, POUR THE MIXTURE INTO A LARGE

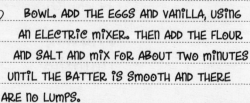

BOWL. ADD THE EGGS AND VANILLA, USING

AN ELECTRIC MIXER. THEN ADD THE FLOUR

AND SALT AND MIX FOR ABOUT TWO MINUTES

UNTIL THE BATTER IS SMOOTH AND THERE

ARE NO LUMPS.

POUR THE BATTER INTO THE GREASED PAN AND BAKE FOR 20-30 MINUTES. USE A TOOTHPICK TO CHECK IF THE BROWNIES ARE DONE—IF THE TOOTHPICK COMES OUT WITH A COUPLE CRUMBS ON IT, THE BROWNIES ARE READY!

LET THEM COOL IN THE PAN.

WHILE THE BROWNIES ARE COOLING, MAKE THE FROSTING!

FROSTING:
1/2 STICK OF BUTTER, SOFTENED
1 CUP OF POWDERED SUGAR

2 TABLESPOONS OF MILK
1/4 TEASPOON OF PEPPERMINT EXTRACT

WITH AN ELECTRIC MIXER, COMBINE ALL INGREDIENTS. IF THE ICING SEEMS TOO THICK OR STIFF, ADD A LITTLE MORE MILK. IF IT'S TOO RUNNY, ADD MORE POWDERED SUGAR.

WHEN THE BROWNIES ARE COOL AND THE FROSTING IS DONE, SPREAD THE FROSTING ON TOP OF THE BROWNIES.

YOU'LL HAVE TO KEEP THE BROWNIES IN THE FRIDGE BECAUSE THE FROSTING HAS BUTTER IN IT—IF YOU CAN KEEP THEM AROUND THAT LONG!

chicken parmigiana

this is my dad's recipe. It's really easy, and really good, too!

4 chicken cutlets
1 egg
1/2 cup dry bread crumbs
1 jar of tomato sauce (12-16 ounces)
1/2 cup shredded mozzarella cheese
1/4 cup grated Parmesan cheese

Preheat the oven to 350 degrees and lightly grease a glass baking dish.
Beat the egg with a whisk. Dip each cutlets into the beaten egg, letting the excess egg mixture drip off.
Now coat the cutlets with breadcrumbs.
Arrange each chicken cutlet in the baking dish and bake for 20-25 minutes.
then pour the tomato sauce over the cutlets and sprinkle the mozzarella

and Parmesan cheese on top. Bake for 15 more minutes, until the sauce is bubbling and the cheese is melted and golden brown on top.

MOZZARELLA

this is really yummy served with a green salad and garlic bread! It's also really good with a side dish of pasta.

—shawn

Fortune Cookies

Fortune cookies aren't Chinese, but they are yummy and fun to make—especially with your friends!

2 egg whites
1/4 teaspoon vanilla extract
1 pinch of salt
1/2 cup white flour
1/2 cup white sugar

First, write your fortunes on small strips of paper (about 1/4 inch wide and 2 inches long).

Then preheat the oven to 400 degrees and butter a cookie sheet.

Carefully separate the egg white from the yolk (have an adult show you how if you've never done this before—it's kind of tricky at first!). Mix the egg whites and the vanilla until the egg whites are foamy, but not stiff.

Then sift the salt, flour, and sugar into the egg and vanilla. Mix well.

Pour a teaspoon of batter onto the cookie sheet for each cookie, and move the sheet around so the batter forms circles. Only try 2 or 3 at first, because you have to fold the cookie up while it's still hot! Once they cool, they get hard and then it's too late!

Bake the cookies for about 5 minutes or until they are golden brown on the edges.

Remove the cookies from the oven and quickly transfer them to a wooden cutting board with a spatula.

Place a fortune in the middle of the cookie, then fold the cookie in half, pressing the edges together so they are sealed.

Fold the cookie in half the other way so that the points meet,

then let it cool in a muffin pan. If the cookie is too hot for you to fold, it might be easier if you wear a pair of clean cotton gloves to protect your fingers. After all the cookies are baked and folded, you can eat them up! Yum!

YOU WILL BE A SUCCESSFUL CHEF

YOU HAVE A GREAT WEALTH OF FRIENDS

MANY ADVENTURES LIE AH

YOU WILL COOK ON T.V. SOMEDAY

149

Cooking Tips from the Chef Girls!

The Chef Girls are looking out for you!
Here are some things you should
know if you want to cook.
(Remember to ask your parents
if you can use knives and the stove!)

1 Tie back long hair so that it won't
get into the food or in the way as
you work.

2 Don't wear loose-fitting clothing
that could drag in the food or
on the stove burners.

3 Never cook in bare feet or open-toed
shoes. Something sharp or hot could
drop on your feet.

4 Always wash your hands before you
handle food.

5 Read through the recipe before you start. Gather your ingredients together and measure them before you begin.

6 Turn pot handles in so that they won't get knocked off the stove.

7 Use wooden spoons to stir hot liquids. Metal spoons can become very hot.

8 When cutting or peeling food, cut away from your hands.

9 Cut food on a cutting board, not the countertop.

10 Hand someone a knife with the knifepoint pointing to the floor.

11 Clean up as you go. It's safer and neater.

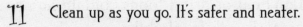

12 Always use a dry pot holder to remove something hot from the oven. You could get burned with a wet one, since wet ones retain heat.

13 Make sure that any spills on the floor are cleaned up right away, so that you don't slip and fall.

14 Don't put knives in clean-up water. You could reach into the water and cut yourself.

15 Use a wire rack to cool hot baking dishes to avoid scorch marks on the countertop.

An Important Message from the Chef Girls!

Some foods can carry bacteria, such as salmonella, that can make you sick.
To avoid salmonella, always cook poultry, ground beef, and eggs thoroughly before eating.
Don't eat or drink foods containing raw eggs.
And wash hands, kitchen work surfaces, and utensils with soap and water immediately after they have been in contact with raw meat or poultry.

mooretimes2: Molly and Amanda

qtpie490: Shawn

happyface: Peichi

BrooklynNatasha: Natasha

JustMac: Justin

Wuzzup: What's up?

Mwa smooching sound

G2G: Got To Go

deets: details

b-b: Bye-Bye

brb: be right back

<3 hearts

L8R: Later, as in "See ya later!"

LOL: Laughing Out Loud

GMTA: Great Minds Think Alike

j/k: Just kidding

B/C: because

W8: Wait

W8 4 me @: Wait for me at

thanx: thanks

BK: Big kiss

MAY: Mad about you

RUF2T?: Are you free to talk?

TTUL: Type to you later

E-ya: will e-mail you

LMK: Let me know

GR8: Great

WFM: Works for me

2: to, too, two

C: see

u: you

2morrow: tomorrow

VH: virtual hug

BFFL: Best Friends For Life

:-@ shock

:-P sticking out tongue

%-) confused

:-o surprised

;-) winking or teasing

dish chicken soup

friends, cooking, eating, talking, life.

We love Mom's homemade chicken soup in the winter—especially when anyone in the family gets a cold or the flu! Homemade chicken soup tastes better than that stuff from a can. It's good for you, too!

First, ask an adult if you can use the stove! An adult should be in the kitchen while you are making this.

8 cups cold water
1 whole chicken (or 3-4 pounds of chicken parts—including bones!)
1 onion, diced

3 cloves garlic, minced
1 bay leaf
1 pound carrots, diced
1 pound celery, diced

1 teaspoon salt
1 teaspoon pepper
½ cup rice, pasta, or orzo
OR matzoh balls

Put the chicken into a large pot and cover with cold water. Bring to a boil, then turn down the heat to a simmer. Add the bay leaf and salt. Simmer the chicken for about three hours until the meat falls off the bones. When the chicken broth is cool, remove the chicken from the pot. Carefully remove the skin and cut the meat into bite-sized pieces. Throw away the skin, bones, and bay leaf. Put the chicken bites in a separate dish and refrigerate. Refrigerate the broth for a few hours or until the fat has risen to the top of the pot. Skim the fat off and throw it away. then strain the broth. Return the broth to the stovetop on medium heat. Add the chicken meat, carrots, celery, onion, and garlic. Simmer until the vegetables are tender. Half an hour before serving, add the rice, pasta, orzo, or matzoh balls. When the rice or pasta is cooked, the soup is ready to serve!

Matzoh Balls

4 eggs
2 tablespoons vegetable oil
½ cup club soda

1 cup matzoh meal
1 teaspoon salt
½ teaspoon pepper (optional)
½ teaspoon onion powder (optional)

I love matzoh ball soup! It's really just chicken soup with matzoh balls, but it's my favorite way to eat chicken soup. Matzoh balls are like dumplings. They are made of matzoh meal. Club soda makes the matzoh balls really light and fluffy!

Whisk the eggs with a fork. Stir the oil and club soda into the eggs. Then mix in the matzoh meal and the salt (and the pepper and onion powder if you are using it). The mixture will be really sticky! When all the ingredients are combined, refrigerate for at least one hour.

When you are ready to cook the matzoh balls, fill a pot with cold water and bring it to a boil. Take the mixture out of the fridge. Then get your hands wet! This will keep the matzoh balls from sticking to your hands, and it will make them easier to form. (My mom always keeps a little bowl of water nearby so she can get her hands wet while she forms the dough into balls.) Take a tablespoon of the matzoh mixture and roll it between your palms so that it forms a ball (don't use too much, because the matzoh balls will puff up when they cook!). When all of the matzoh balls are made, **CAREFULLY** drop them into the boiling water. Cover and cook for 30 minutes (if you are not having them in soup, cook the matzoh balls for 45 minutes). Remove the matzoh balls from the boiling water, and gently simmer them in chicken soup for the last fifteen minutes. Then your matzoh ball soup will be ready! Yum!

From dish #6: On the Back Burner. Published by Grosset & Dunlap, a division of Penguin Putnam Books for Young Readers. Text copyright © 2003 by Diane Muldrow. Illustrations copyright © 2003 by Barbara Pollak.